Anthology of Possibilities

David Reynolds-Moreton

sci-fi-cafe.com

Anthology of Possibilities
David Reynolds-Moreton

This edition Copyright © 2022 by Oxford eBooks Ltd.
Published under the sci-fi-cafe.com imprint.
www.oxford-ebooks.com
Story Copyright © 1998 by David Reynolds-Moreton

The right of the author to be identified as the author of this work
has been asserted in accordance with the
Copyright, Designs and Patents Act 1988.

All characters and events in this book are fictitious.
Any resemblance to any person living or dead is purely coincidental.

All rights reserved.
No part of this publication may be reproduced, stored in a retrieval system, or
transmitted, in any form or by any means, electronic, mechanical, photocopying,
recording or otherwise, without the prior permission of the copyright owners.

ISBN 978-1-910-779-89-7(Paperback)

sci-fi-cafe.com

Fourteen short stories of various possibilities. Read them with an open mind. Do not reject something out of unthinking option. Just a thought - remember, that which you resist, you become the effect of, to the degree that you resist it! - Enjoy. (DBRM)

FOR WANT OF A BREATH
JUST BECAUSE YOU CAN'T
LANDFILL SOLUTION
THE SEA
THE WARPING STONES
CHANGELING
A HUMAN AILMENT
THE PLANTING
MOVING ON
THE STEPS
EXCHANGLING
THE RETURN
FROM LONG AGO
OLD AND NEW BITS

FOR WANT OF BREATH

THE TROUBLES BEGAN in the latter months of 2018. The Pacific Ocean surface temperature rose by point eight of a degree C above that which was normal, resulting in the worst El Niño effect on record. The torrential rains in some parts of the world caused the worst flooding in living memory, while other parts suffered droughts of unimaginable intensity.

The raging floods washed huge amounts of soil, along with its natural and artificial fertilizers, into the rivers, and then down to the sea. Slurry pits from coastal farms and sewerage works overflowed uncontrollably, adding to the nitrogen and phosphorous pollution of the coastal waters.

The droughts which swept through the poorer nations had a devastating effect, as plants withered and died, quickly followed by the livestock on which the population relied for food. Aid could not be sent in quickly enough to stop millions dying from starvation, while what little that was normally exported to support those countries, failed, adding to the problem.

When the pollution in the sea water reached a certain level, the algae blooms began. Algae blooms occur quite naturally, and normally cause no problems; but due to the high concentration of pollutants, these blooms were massive, colouring great patches of the oceans and were even visible from space.

Fish stocks were decimated from the toxins released from the blooms, and those peoples who relied on fish as a major part of their diet were hardest hit. The only fish available were from those few patches of ocean which the blooms had not as yet reached, namely the Polar Regions, so only those who were rich enough were able to eat fish. The disruption to the fishing industry world wide was cataclysmic, and with the industry on the point of collapse, some means of combating the blooms was sought.

Experiments went ahead looking for something which would kill, or at least control, the blooms. The main line of research was along the lines of a virus, which could be sprayed from aircraft. Many in the scientific community thought this was too dangerous to use, as they were not satisfied the virus would be selective enough, and could possibly kill off all the cyanobacteria which produces most of our atmospheric oxygen.

With worldwide conditions worsening, caution was thrown to the winds, and the spraying began. It seemed to be successful, with the blooms of algae gradually decreasing, and the oceans slowly returning to their normal colour. However, the effectiveness of the virus had been wildly underestimated, as it continued to remove more algae than was intended.

From samples of seawater taken at regular intervals to check conditions, it is thought, but not yet proven, that due to some coastal nuclear reactors illegally releasing radioactive water into the sea, the virus had mutated and had run out of control.

As most of our oxygen comes from photosynthesis (land based plants and ocean born cyanobacteria), concerns were growing as to what would happen if the virus should destroy all the oxygen producing bacteria in the ocean, as already the extreme droughts and the fires which followed them, had destroyed so much of the Earth's plant life; and oxygen was not being replaced in sufficient quantities according to some scientists.

It was some long time later when the first effects of lower oxygen levels were noticed. Those with chronic breathing problems found their difficulties were exacerbated by the drop in oxygen concentration, similar to what a normal person would experience as altitude sickness. Those who were in serious difficulties, and who couldn't get supplementary oxygen, died.

Slowly, the Earth's over population brought about by man's own disregard for the effects of his own greed, and lack of consideration for the planet's wellbeing, was being adjusted.

Extraction of oxygen from the air increased alarmingly as the demand for supplementary supplies grew, some large department stores even adding extra oxygen to the atmosphere of their buildings as a way of bringing more customers in.

As there was no sign of the oceans recovering from their depletion of oxygen supplying algae, and the population still dropping, thoughts turned to searching out any surviving algae and creating oxygen generating plants using organic waste.

The first plants worked quite well, although the amounts produced were more academic than useful, so gene manipulation got underway to produce a more vigorous strain. Meanwhile, most of the major governments got together to ban unnecessary burning of fossil fuel, and tree planting was implemented on a huge scale.

When the first super algae came on stream, they were used in plants situated in large buildings to improve the wellbeing of those inside, as just bleeding the oxygen into the atmosphere was deemed pointless because of the dilution in such a vast volume.

The system was quite simple in reality. Organic waste was collected in large volumes, nothing went to waste. Some oxygen from the atmosphere was used in converting the waste into a usable form, and it was processed to produce a liquid rich in nutrients for the super algae to feed on, the oxygen so produced was either fed into the building's air supply, or compressed and stored for when it was needed. In actual fact, very little was actually stored, as industry needed large supplies for some of its processes.

Still the Earth's population declined, mainly in the poorer countries that were unable to manufacture the oxygen producing plants in sufficient quantities, and those in remote regions stood no chance. Anyone with breathing problems or in poor health had little hope of surviving.

Various quasi religious sects sprang up in desperate populations, blaming the scientists and industrialists for calling down the wrath of God upon them, having little scientific knowledge on which to base their beliefs. Things got very unpleasant for a while, with several buildings related to science being set on fire, and a rash of murders.

Some degree of stability was restored after a number of radio and video broadcasts explained what had caused the catastrophe, but general mismanagement of governments was not entirely let off the hook.

Some years after the oxygenating plants had been established in most large buildings and factories; small private house owners were unable to afford them, and found life getting even more difficult as oxygen levels dropped even further.

The oxygen generating plants continued to improve, as did new strains of the super algae - just in time for man's greatest attempt yet to handle the situation.

The first purpose-built enclosed city came into being a few years later, followed by many others in those countries which had the necessary funds. In countries with little infrastructure or the financial means to build these safe havens, life just got worse, causing attempted migration wherever possible. Sadly, most of those who had coped to some degree could not accept the influx, as it would overwhelm their already carefully balanced systems. Many lives were sadly lost in the attempt.

Strict birth control was imposed in the cities, limiting each family to only produce enough children to replace their parents. Some religions fought against the idea to begin with, but when given the ultimatum that they toe the line or try life outside the city; they had little alternative.

Slowly the Earth began to recover, as the plants which had survived used the extra carbon dioxide in the atmosphere to expand into any area which had sufficient rainfall. Many animals were lost for ever, but those which had struggled through the catastrophe began to slowly multiply. The oceans were to all intents and purposes dead. Those fish which survived were not economically harvestable, and it had been decided not to fish the oceans until such time as fish stocks had returned to near normal.

It was not too long before all humanity was living in enclosed cities, only going outside to tend the fields, equipped with breathing masks. Those who had lived high up on the mountains and were used to the rarefied air, moved down to the lowlands, and survived to some degree, although life was not easy.

Meanwhile, research had been going on apace to create algae to replenish the oceans oxygenating properties. The virus which had got out of control was no longer present, as far as the scientists could tell, and now huge enclosures of sea water were used to test each new mutation of the algae as it was discovered.

By now, Earth's population had dropped to about one eighth of its former numbers, and with the strict birth control laws firmly in place and agreed to by most, looked as if it would stabilise.

At long last, the researchers constructed an algae which multiplied quickly in sea water and produced oxygen efficiently, but could they control it once it had been released? Tests in the massive sea water enclosures looked hopeful.

The ensuing row between governments about the release of the new algae went on for some time, as there was no way of proving that the release wouldn't cause even more problems. Several more tests were done, controlling the nutriment levels in the test lagoons to see if the algae would mutate when nutriment levels fell below that which was necessary to sustain the colony, and what happened when an excess of nutriment was introduced. All the tests proved positive, to the satisfaction of most of the governments, but not all, and so production of vast quantities of the algae went ahead.

The Atlantic Ocean was the first to be seeded, and regular water tests were carried out which backed up the scientists' predictions - the algae spread as they had forecast, but it would be some time before oxygen levels would rise enough to be measured, and confirm the success of the project.

The next step which indicated that humankind had restored a degree of sanity to its operations, was the formation of a world government. There were many objections, but common sense prevailed in the end, and the serious business of sustained existence was underway. It was the fact that so many of the world's population had at last realised how close they had come to the extinction of the human race through their unregulated folly, that clinched the deal. Fair trading regulations, with a common currency, and coupled with strict birth control, held the whole system together.

There were many objections from some religious organisations about population control, but there always had been. These were, fairly or unfairly, depending upon your view point, overruled for the good of all.

Many animal species seemed to have adopted to the low levels of oxygen, mutating over several generations, those who had a slight genetic advantage to low oxygen levels, survived, to breed more of their kind, while those lacking this change failed to breed.

It will be a long time before man would be able to roam over his home world as in days of old, it will take a long time for the oxygen levels in the atmosphere to return to normal. At long last, a period resembling sanity was in place, and with strict control, would ensure that mankind and its home planet would survive into the distant future.

JUST BECAUSE YOU CAN'T

AN INVITATION WAS sent out to all the top ranking physicists to attend a very important demonstration - all expenses paid, and a jolly good lunch. The hall was crowded by two o'clock, and a few extra chairs had to be brought in and set up in the aisles to accommodate latecomers.

At two-thirty the doors were closed, and locked. The general hubbub died down as a smart suited middle aged man took up his position on the stage.

'I would like to thank you all for attending this meeting - I don't think you will be disappointed by the time I have finished this afternoon. My name is Julian Bradshaw, and I am the Director for Physical Research at this campus. You will see two pieces of film - the first was taken on a mobile phone, and camerawork not great. A high quality video camera was used for the second, and what you will see is exactly as it was recorded - there has been no camera trickery or CGI involved - please bear this in mind during the viewing. If you are all ready, the first film will be shown, and I will narrate as there is no sound track.'

The lights dimmed, and the beam of a projector burst from somewhere at the back of the hall. The screen showed a work bench with a square metal frame lying on top of it. The frame had a collection of small boxes arranged on its surface, linked together with coloured wires, and a thick wire hung down from overhead in a loop to join one of the boxes.

'I am told that this is an attempt at achieving anti-gravity,' the Director said. 'And as we all know, according to the laws of physics as they are now, this is impossible. So please watch closely.'

Two men in white coats came into view; one adjusted something on one of the boxes, looked at a hand held instrument, and nodded his head. They both stepped back so that they were only just in view, and the other man pressed a button on a small control box in his hand.

The metal plate with the boxes seemed to shimmer slightly, and then rose up into the air by about two metres, gently rocking to and fro for a moment, and then settled down to hover quite still above the table.

'You will notice,' the Director interjected, 'that the cable supplying power to the device is still hanging in a loop, so it is in no way supporting the plate - and just in case you are thinking of a magnetic field, we don't have a magnet powerful enough to push the plate up two metres.'

One of the men did something to the control box in his hand and the metal plate accelerated upwards, punching a hole in the ceiling - there was a bright flash, and the film ended.

'I would just like to point out one thing,' said the Director. 'You will have noticed the plate knocked a hole in the ceiling - if it was just anti-gravity, the plate would have simply hit the ceiling and then stayed there - I think we have something else here, but what it is, I have no idea.'

As the screen went blank, and after a stunned silence, everyone began talking at once. The Director had to make several attempts to get the attention of the audience.

'I only have it by word of mouth, but in the ensuing explosion both technicians were injured, and one died later, also the workshop was wrecked, and there was nothing left of the equipment they were experimenting with. The second film was taken sometime later, and I would assume that the remaining experimenter was the one who flies the device, and knows how it was made. We will show that film now.'

Again the projector lit the screen, and this time the scene was out in the open. A metal platform about half a metre thick with a hand rail and control box attached, lay on the grass. Three white coated men stood around it, while a third man came into view wearing a jump suit and helmet. He stepped onto the platform, waved to his companions, did something to the control panel, and the device slowly floated upwards to about five metres - and hung there - with no visible means of suspension or support.

After a few moments, the platform wobbled a bit - a small puff of smoke was seen to leave the base of the platform, and then it accelerated upwards to disappear into the cloud base. The film continued for a few minutes longer, the white coated men standing there looking up into the sky with shocked expressions on their faces - and then the film ended.

This time there was a stunned silence as the Director gained the stage.

'The sole purpose of showing you these two pieces of film is to illustrate the fact that what we thought was impossible can actually happen. The laws of physics will have to be looked at again, and possibly rewritten to some extent.

The three men on the ground, I am informed, were merely helpers, and know nothing of the workings of the device. So far, we have not been able to trace any information or drawings, and although the workshop has been located, there was nothing in it to help us determine how the device worked.

The only piece of information I do have, is that it was powered by Lithium Ion batteries - apart from that, we have nothing. The man on the platform and the device itself have never been found, and believe me, we have looked.

Gentlemen - we now know it can be done, and we owe it to that brave man who is probably dead, to find out how. I wish you all good fortune in your research - thank you.'

The Director left the stage in a hushed silence. Sometime later, one of the faculty members, who was a personal friend, asked the Director what was the real purpose of the film show, somehow sensing something was not quite right, to which he replied,

'You must keep this strictly to yourself. The films of course were faked, despite what I said - I think the ends justify the means, if you see what I mean. I consider we are too hidebound by convention - we have lost the ability to research the impossible, and that is where progress lies. If just some of them are convinced, they will approach the subject of anti-gravity from a different angle - and who knows, we may well achieve it.'

THE LANDFILL SOLUTION

I LOVE MESSING about with electronics - always have done, and sometimes I come up with something really useful - even make a little money to keep me in beer and smokes, and the odd Cartier watch.

One day, I noticed that a circuit was drawing a lot more power than I had anticipated - in fact the ammeter needle had slammed right across the dial and was quivering, trying to get past the stop pin. The power supply 'limit' light had come on - and that rarely happens.

Let me explain - the power supply drops the mains voltage down to twelve volts, or whatever I choose. There is a current limiting device built in, so that if I make a mistake, the whole thing doesn't catch fire - or blow up. The 'limit' light comes on if the circuit I am using draws too much current, and warns me of the fact.

I doubled the 'limit' threshold, and found the circuit was still drawing one hell of a lot of power, but nothing was heating up - there should have been a wisp of smoke at least. So where was all that current going? After checking all the components for over heating, and finding nothing untoward, I could feel the hair on the back of my neck rising. Was this another strange discovery? The power was going somewhere - but where?

Hitching up a coil of wire to the output of the circuit, I put the power on again and noticed a very slight shimmer around the coil. Perhaps it was generating a massive electric field? Only way to find out was to drop a piece of iron into the coil, and see what happened. Where's a piece of old iron when you want it? - I found a bent nail on the floor and dropped it into the coil - and the nail disappeared. A copper washer with a bit of chewing gum attached was next, and that vanished - even the gum. A scrunched up sweet wrapper and an apple core followed, with the same result.

Somehow the coil was sending these objects somewhere - but where?

A metre long piece of wood, which looked as if it would just about fit inside the coil, was held above it - and dropped. The wood just fell into the coil, and was no more. This was something else!

The circuit was meticulously copied down - some bits didn't make much sense, in fact I began to wonder why I had put them there in the first place.

That afternoon, I cleared my workshop of all the junk and rubbish which had accumulated over the years, breaking up some of the bigger pieces, and feeding them into my new rubbish disposal unit.

Didn't sleep much that night, wondering how I could make some cash out of the device - and then the penny dropped, as they say.

The normal waste disposal service took care of most household rubbish, but if you wanted to get rid of bulk or large items, it cost. Bingo!

Next day I built a really big coil, some two metres across; hitched it up to the electronics and moved the whole lot outside, attaching an extension lead from my workshop. There were some lumps of rock left over from the new rockery construction, so those went in - didn't even hit the ground beneath the coil. An old bicycle frame - minus a wheel, a broken garden chair (plastic) and a pile of old bricks followed - into oblivion, but I was a little concerned as to where it was going. Nothing actually disappears - the law of conservation of energy states that, so it was going somewhere.

I went to the neighbours either side and said I was getting rid of some bulk items, and if they would like to bring their waste around to my garden, I'd add it to mine.

The disposal unit was covered with a piece of canvas, no point in showing anyone what was going on just yet. A couple of hours later, and I had a sizeable pile of rubbish to test the machine with. It all disappeared - I was in business.

I realised I would have to think this through carefully. First I would hire an old warehouse somewhere, install a larger version of the gadget with a hopper so that things could be just thrown in without hitting the coil - and then tout for business.

Just in case anything went wrong, or I was breaking the law, I adopted a disguise. A very convincing wig, dark glasses and a moustache, with a complete change of clothing when operating the 'waste disposal unit', seemed to have everything covered.

A quick visit to the local private waste collectors, with a printed sheet, a map and charges per load, the starting date, and things were ready to go. I had already set up a new bank account with a different name, and that was a bit tricky, although I expected most payments would be in cash - that's how the trade works.

On the first day of operations, I was at the warehouse early, checking out the conveyor which would take the rubbish into the building and then on to the 'coil'. No one could see what was going on inside, but I hadn't thought of an explanation of how I would send the waste on to somewhere else.

Eight o'clock sharp, and the first lorry arrived - builders waste, mainly broken bricks, old bits of timber and the odd concrete block, along with an assortment of large tins. The conveyor groaned a bit, but it all went in, and when the lorry left I went in through a side door to see how the unit had coped. No sign of anything amiss, so I patted the wad of cash in my pocket, and went outside ready for the next load, which wasn't long in coming.

It wasn't hard work really, all I had to do was make sure the lorry was in the correct position, and then switch the conveyor on - and take the money of course.

A huge truck arrived mid week, loaded with old unwanted furniture from a private recycling centre. 'What do you do with it all?' asked the driver.

'I have a special compactor in there, and it squashes everything down to almost nothing - then it's just a matter of taking the compressed blocks to the usual disposal depot. It works out a lot cheaper if it's compressed, hence my low rate to you,' I lied.

Three weeks into the project, and the amount of cash was getting a bit embarrassing, with only a few cheques to bank, but they were big ones.

I did wonder when someone would come snooping around to see what was going on, but so far, no one had. That wouldn't last for long though.

In the third month of operation, there was a long queue of assorted lorries and trucks all down the road, right up to the junction of the main highway. I knew I would be in trouble if this continued - someone would get upset, possibly the traffic police, and I didn't have a licence to operate a waste disposal unit from the local council anyway.

Luckily, someone saw an opportunity, and grabbed it. I had a visit from some smart suited gentlemen from an international company in the same trade. Someone had been keeping watch on the warehouse, and noticed that nothing left it. The game was up, I could no longer keep the secret of the 'coil' to myself - and I knew it.

They didn't mess about. They came straight to the point - show them how it worked, or there could be problems, so show them I did. The look on their collective faces was something I will never forget. You could see the cash signs rolling up as they realised the potential of my invention - and they wanted to buy it. I had little option really, but I did build in some 'safety' factors. There were several more visits, lots of haggling, and then the final offer. It was a mind boggling sum. I would supply the electronics - they would build the coils, and all the rest of the equipment, and as I wouldn't give them the circuit details, I had to just about sign my life away that I would never divulge the secret to anyone else - or else! They didn't say 'terminal' in as many words, but I knew what they meant.

I enclosed the electronics in a solid block of thermo setting resin reinforced with glass fibre, with terminals for the power input, and another set for the output to the coil; thus making it very difficult for anyone to take it apart and see how it worked. I was taken to one of their main sites, where a massive new building had been set up, and everything was ready for the addition of the 'circuit' block. I connected it up, and switched on the power - and the first load of rubbish went down the chute - to somewhere else.

Having satisfied the Company that my device did the job, they handed over the cheque - it was a whopper, but considering what they would make out of the device in the years to come - they had the better end of the bargain.

Always careful to have an escape route or backup scheme, I had set up several accounts, so that the money could be shuffled around and 'lost', making it very difficult to trace where it had gone. The final resting place was in a Swiss bank, and only I could get at it.

I always wore my disguise when meeting anyone from the Company or visiting the site - I was ready to 'disappear' should the need ever arise. Forward planning always pays off, as I was about to discover some weeks later.

I was on my way to make one last visit to the disposal plant before 'disappearing' into retirement, and stopped on top of a nearby hill to look at the scene - don't know why, I just did. The plant was going at full belt, a long stream of lorries were queuing up to dump their loads of rubbish into the chutes leading to the 'coil'. They had improved the setup by having two chutes feeding into the building, so as one lorry was leaving, another was at the second chute dumping its load. I wondered if the 'coil' could take the strain of so much stuff being put through it, but it seemed to be coping.

And then it happened. The roof of the building shot up into the air, followed by a stream of detritus rising up some fifty metres, and climbing. Gravity then began to take effect, the top mushroomed out, and the whole mighty column came crashing down, but the hole in the roof continued to pour forth more rubbish. Within seconds, it seemed the whole of the building was covered, and disappeared from sight under a growing mound - and still the column of junk jetted skywards.

Someone, somewhere, didn't want our rubbish, and was sending it back - and how! Even from where I was, I could hear the low rumble as countless tons of our unwanted items were being returned - and then, just as the column died down a little, there was a flash, and a muffled explosion as the coil and driving electronics gave up the unequal struggle, and disintegrated.

There was now a massive mountain of junk towering up into the sky where the disposal unit had been, and little wisps of smoke began to rise as burnable items reacted to the heat released from the now defunct electronics.

As I said earlier, forward planning pays off. I got back into my car and drove off, not too fast, but fast enough to leave the area before anyone else arrived to see what had happened. The car was left on the edge of an old quarry which was full of water. I removed my disguise and burnt it, took the folding bike from the boot, and giving the car a hefty push, saw the other 'me' disappear for good.

I am now on a beach in the lovely warm sunshine - not too hot - just pleasant. I have a very nice little house just a few metres away, a smart car, and two servants. I'm not saying where I am, that remains a secret, along with the details of the 'coil' and it's driving electronics - it might come in useful again one day - if I ever run out of money, but that doesn't seem likely.

THE SEA

THEY WERE SWIMMING along about ten metres off the shore line, their heads above water, laughing and splashing each other when Kim called out,

'Hey Sukie, look, there's one of those strange creatures, haven't seen one for a long time; it seems to be looking for something.'

Sukie increased speed to catch up with him, raising her head well above the small wavelets as they gently flowed in to break on the beach.

'My father said his father told him that once upon a time there were many of them. They used to come down to lie on the sand, and gaze out to sea. I wonder why they did that?'

'Don't know, anyway, there aren't many of them now. Could be due to the lack of green stuff at the top of the beach - it's all brown and dry now, never used to be.'

The pair swam on until they were level with the creature, who then bent down, picked up a pebble and threw it at them.

'That's not nice,' said Sukie, ducking under the water, 'I wonder why they do that?'

'Maybe it's because they're hungry,' Kim replied, 'and that makes them angry. We'd get angry if we didn't have anything to eat, or at least, I would.'

They stayed there for a while, treading water and watching the creature as it roamed about on the sand, stooping down every now and again to pick something up, sniff it, and then discard it.

'What do you think it's looking for?' asked Sukie.

'Maybe something to eat, it looks very thin, and wobbles about as it walks. I wouldn't mind giving it some fish, but it would probably just throw stones at us.'

The thin creature on the beach armed itself with several large pebbles, and then staggered down to the waters edge. As the first pebbles hit the water near them, the two dolphins turned as one and quickly swam out of range.

THE WARPING STONES

What follows below is a reprint from an old diary found in a box of junk bought at a car boot sale in 1972. We have been unable to trace the author, but thought it might stir a few memories - if you know of the individual who wrote this, please get in touch with the publisher.

IN 1965 I took early retirement from my job in London, and having spent several holidays in Devon, decided to live there, as I enjoyed walking the moors.

I am writing this record of my experience, as I do not understand how such a thing can have happened.

I had just had lunch at the Church House Inn in the little hamlet of Holne, and asked about the old tin working I had heard about. They suggested that if I follow an old track called Sandy Way, I should come across it.

Part way along the track were two granite gateposts, an odd place to put them, I thought - maybe there had been a wall here in the distant past, but it was long gone now. Without thinking, I passed between them and felt a slight *shimmer* - I don't know how else to describe it - but then it was gone, and I continued my walk.

It was a very pleasant afternoon, with a cool breeze blowing to take the edge off the blazing heat of the summer sun. In the distance I could see some stone buildings, and a wisp of smoke coming from one of them. I was surprised, as I had been told the old working had been abandoned long ago, and only the ruins remained.

As I drew nearer, I could clearly hear men's voices and the faint clatter of machinery; and instead of being grass covered, the track was now one of small stones, and well worn. Looking around, I was surprised to see about fifteen men doing various jobs - at the pub they said the old tin working had been closed a long time ago, perhaps this was another tin working.

As I neared the building with the smoke coming out of its chimney, a man pushing an old fashioned wooden wheelbarrow came around the corner.

'Good afternoon,' I said, but he totally ignored me, as if I hadn't been there - perhaps he was deaf, I thought - but he must have seen me. I approached two other men who were shovelling some pieces of black rock into a small wheeled truck, but neither looked up as I bid them the time of day - it was almost as if I was invisible to them - and later, this proved to be the case.

For some inexplicable reason, they couldn't see or hear me, and then I realised, they were all dressed as if they belonged to the past century. For one moment I thought the impossible had happened, and had I gone back in time. But I was still dressed in my normal clothes, so that couldn't be the case. As I couldn't make contact with any of the men, I wandered around the site and watched them at work for a while, and then continued my walk. The track had now disappeared, so I dropped down to follow the river Mardle, a small stream really, but there must have been a path here at sometime, as the bank was clear and made walking easy.

The normal gorse and bracken soon gave way to what I think is called scrub oak, small stunted oak trees, the branches of those near the stream being draped in hanging moss like strands. Just ahead, in a clearing, I could see a large and a small hut, both composed of a ring of very neatly placed rocks about three feet high, and capped with a cone shaped roof of what looked like rushes. A man dressed in animal skins was sitting outside one of the huts, skinning a rabbit or some other small animal.

I called out to him, but he didn't even look up - so I suppose I was invisible to him as well. I walked up to the hut and looked into a hole in the stone wall; a fire was smouldering in the centre within a circle of stones and opposite was a pile of bracken with a shape nestled in it, but it was too dark to see any details. I've just realised - my eyes didn't sting from the smoke.

I went over to the other smaller hut, and looked in through a small hole in the wall; little light penetrated into the gloomy interior, so all I could make out were several woven baskets hanging from the roof beams.

Leaving the huts, I followed the stream a little further, but it was getting colder now, with hints of frost on the ground, and in the distance I could see a bank of snow. I didn't feel the cold, so I carried on. The stream was now iced over, with only a trickle of water under it - and then it was solid ice. Ahead, towering blocks of blue tinted ice barred my way up the valley. It was at this point that the realisation fully sunk in - I had somehow travelled back in time, and this was the ice age - or something very like it.

To one side of the ice cliff, some of it had broken away, and it looked as though I could perhaps climb up through the tumble of ice blocks if I had some climbing equipment with me - I just had to see what was on the other side. I checked my watch - it was time I was getting back to the real world, not knowing when night would fall here.

I hurried back down the valley, past the huts (no sign of the man) and past the tin mine - the men were still working, and then the stony track turned to grass and I knew I was back in the real world. I was very tempted to call in at the pub and tell them what I had found, but as I intended to eat there again, I thought better of it.

Driving home, I began to doubt what I had seen - perhaps it was something I had eaten? No, it was too real; I would have to get some climbing gear and return.

Sleep didn't come easily that night, and it was several days later before I managed to obtain the necessary climbing equipment. The weather was still holding good, although once I had entered the 'past' it didn't seem to matter - I just seemed to feel comfortable - even at the ice barrier. I stocked up with all the rations I could carry, including a small tent and a wind up torch. I wanted to take a gun, but remembering that I didn't seem to impinge on the 'past' world, there was little point in taking one.

After a good protein breakfast, and armed with two walking poles, I set off, leaving my car in the pub car park, and headed up the grassy track. It was with some relief when the grass turned to stones, and the sounds of the mining operation drifted down in the cool morning air.

There was no one in the huts, but the fire was still smouldering - so I assumed the occupants were out hunting for their breakfast.

The ice wall was just the same as it had been several days before, and the rift in the frozen cliff beckoned. The lightweight crampons made easy work of the first section, but later I had to make a lasso to haul myself up the last part of the ice wall. The view from the top was amazing. Realising I would have to return this way, I tied a spare brown shirt I had in my backpack to one of the poles to act as a marker for my return.

Looking back the way I had come was disconcerting, to say the least, as it seemed to disappear into a strange mist, which I hadn't noticed before. Ahead, the ice field stretched into the distance for as far as I could see, and I began to wonder if there was any point in going any further; then I remembered that the 'scene' changed quite quickly without my noticing it, so I walked on.

Sure enough, the ice gave way to snow after a while, and then I was back on solid ground. The grass was short and tough looking, and stretched for miles - studded with small groups of odd looking trees. A low growl made me jump - I was a few feet away from a sabre toothed tiger lying out in the shade of a tree from the scorching sun.

Although it couldn't see me, it must have somehow sensed my presence, for it got up, stared me straight in the face and yawned, exposing those two terrible fangs, and then it lay down again. I walked on for a while, and then stopped for a break as my legs were not used to this much continuous work. As I tucked into some biscuits and a rather bent sandwich, I wondered if I left some food the local wild life would eat it? I scattered some broken biscuits on the ground around me, but what few crawling creatures there were just passed them by. Perhaps everything which passed through the stone pillars at the beginning of my journey was rendered invisible to this world.

When I resumed my travels, I found myself in a burned area - everything had been reduced to ashes, and for a while it seemed darkish, with fine dust in the air, but that soon passed and I was out in the open again. The grass was different, if it was grass. In the distance a line of trees stood tall and dark, but unlike any trees I have seen - and then I remembered, I had seen them before, in Kew Gardens tropical house - they were Cycads - and massive.

Suddenly a loud roar rent the otherwise still air, and a huge four legged creature with a long neck came stumbling out of the group of trees, closely followed a giant two legged lizard. I didn't recognise the first dinosaur, but the second one was a Tyrannosaurus Rex. The first dinosaur swung round and went back into the Cycads, hotly pursued by the giant lizard. A terrible scream rent the air; my first instinct was to avoid the area, and then I remembered, I was invisible to them, and was therefore safe.

The cycad forest gave way to an area of giant ferns, and somewhere I could hear the crunching up of bones. It was an unnerving sound, and I couldn't help feel a shudder go through my body. I advanced slowly, and a few yards away I could see something more like a scaly lizard than the dinosaurs I had seen in books. It was busy ripping the flesh off a carcass, swallowing huge chunks without chewing. I wondered if this was the precursor of the dinosaurs - it certainly didn't look like any I had seen before.

The fern forest gave way to what looked more like clumps of moss or lichen, it certainly wasn't grass, and in the distance I could see the glint of water. Going down a slope of gravel and sand, I was confronted by what I presumed was the ocean. Huge waves crashed on the shore, the spray being blown inland by a steady wind. The sky over the ocean had a heavy leaden look, grey and foreboding - I wondered just how far back in time I had travelled, there had been no sign of life for the last few minutes - there wasn't even any seaweed on the miserable looking beach.

Had I reached the point where life hadn't begun on Earth? As I walked along the beach I kept a sharp lookout for anything living - but there was nothing I could see, perhaps life existed in the waters, for that's where it was supposed to have begun.

A short while later I stopped, I now had the feeling that this was a lifeless world, not from what I hadn't seen, but just an irrevocable feeling I had. I don't know why, but I felt sad. I had known such a beautiful world, and this gloomy place was nothing like it.

A shadow passed over me, and I looked up in shock. A massive cylindrical object was slowly floating overhead, some hundreds of feet above me, and heading out to sea. It stopped, and several small spheres left the cylinder and gently floated down to splash into the sea. One of the spheres landed quite near me, a mere few yards from the shore line. I watched fascinated, as the sphere seemed to dissolve before my eyes, releasing a pale brown fluid which quickly dispersed in the water.

Suddenly, a thin beam of light came down from the cylinder, and where it touched the beach, the gravel and sand seemed to glow - and it was heading towards me, so I ran up the beach towards a pile of rocks, and just managed to crawl into a small space between them as the patch of light swept by. I looked up, and couldn't see the cylinder for the rock overhead, so assumed it couldn't see me - but the light continued to roam about outside my hiding place for several minutes before flickering out.

I waited for several minutes more before venturing out of my rocky hiding place. The cylinder had now moved out over the sea some considerable distance, and I could just about make out the little spheres drifting down. I was hungry, having eaten nearly all the food I had brought, and thought it time to return to my own world, or to be more precise, the future, where I belonged.

What amazed me, was the speed with which I travelled, or to put it another way, the distance in time which was spanned in just a short walk. Back on the ice field I wondered if I would be able to find the cleft in the wall of ice up which I had climbed, and which I must go down to return home. After a few minutes, I could see my brown top on the walking pole, flapping in the gentle breeze.

Scrambling down the slippery ice, I was glad to see everything was exactly as it had been on my outward journey, and I hurried on down the valley, past the two round huts, the mine workings, through those two strange stone pillars and so to the pub car park. Back inside my trusty car, I felt safer - this was the world I knew.

After a good meal, I wrote up my notes for the day, but the memory of the cylinder and what it was doing would not leave my mind - I would have to go back and find out, if I could. I decided to return to the beach, find a hiding place, and watch. By moving up and down the beach, I should be able to move about in the time stream, and note any changes which were taking place. I already had a bizarre idea what the cylinder was all about, but I needed proof - and this was the only way to get it.

The excitement was almost too much, but I did eventually get to sleep - and it was the deepest sleep I had ever had - waking up next morning feeling quite refreshed. I packed up some rations and plenty of water, and am now about to set off.

I look forward to writing up what I will find, but if anyone will believe it - that's another matter - it seems too preposterous. Perhaps I could get someone else to come with me - that would be proof indeed. Anyway, I am now setting out for the last part of this adventure - I should be back by early evening.

Here the notes end, with several blank pages following. We have checked very carefully, and no pages have been removed. What happened to him? We don't even have a name, but if anyone recognises the writer, please get in touch.

CHANGELING

I WISH WE could get out of this hell-hole - well, it's not really a hell-hole, it's a beautiful bit of countryside, about ten square miles of it - a river runs through it, there are wooded hills, and it's always summer - except for Christmas, and then it snows - and how. It usually lasts for about four weeks, or until *he* gets bored with it - and then it's gone - just like that!

Sometimes we get the snow in the middle of summer, and that screws up the crops and we all go hungry - except *him*.

The problem is the mist - you can't go through it. It's like white soft spongy stuff - sort of. I tried to push my hand into it one day, and got an electric shock for my trouble. It surrounds the whole place, and keeps us trapped here - otherwise we would have all gone - long ago.

We all live in a little hamlet of cottages - very pretty, and cosy - except they keep changing colour every now and again - and sometimes the doors won't open when we want them to. I was trapped inside for three whole days once - just because I didn't smile at *him* - I always smile now, even when *he's* not looking.

It all started some ten years ago. A young dishevelled woman with long dirty hair came a knocking on Ben's door. He's a nice old guy - heart of gold. He took pity on her, and let her have a room at the back of his cottage. Fed her - got her to wash her hair, and even bought her a new dress one day. And then she developed a bulge. We pulled old Ben's leg something awful - of course he denied it, but his face always went a deep red under his sunburn. We somehow knew he wasn't responsible.

The night she gave birth we had the worst storm in living memory - never seen anything like it, and don't want to again.

Old Molly attended the birth, while Ben was running around with hot water and tearing up some old sheets into neat little squares. The ground shook, and everything not bolted down rattled or fell off its shelf. The lightning flashes were something else, damn near blinded us - and then he appeared. The storm cleared within minutes - couldn't believe it.

Old Guppy, Ben's best friend, paid him a visit a couple of days later - and saw the mother and child, and as he was leaving he quietly muttered to Ben, 'Ugly little sod, isn't he'. Shouldn't have done that - but we didn't know that until later.

Over the next few days, poor old Guppy's hair dropped out, as did

half his teeth, and it looked as if a bullock cart had run over his face
- never seen so many wrinkles and folds. He now walks all bent over,
his eyes water all the time, as does his nose.

It was sometime later that we realised we had to be careful what
we said within ear shot of *him* - but by then it was too late for some.
Jan Brookfield said he was leaving - felt something evil was going on,
'He's a bloody changeling, that's what,' he said. - That's when the mist
appeared - none of us could leave.

We sort of got used to it, had to be careful what we said of course.
It wasn't long before we realised we now had to be self sufficient.
Growing food wasn't too bad, we had done that for ages, but now
there was no going to the nearby town to buy those little extra things
we enjoyed so much.

The old forge hadn't been used since I was a boy. It was now repaired,
and a stock of charcoal built up - couldn't take broken farm machinery
into town for repair any more - luckily, Ben's younger brother Phil,
could remember how it was done, so he got the job.

One winter, the young woman died. She got some sort of infection
- lost a lot of weight - just withered away. Sad really, she was a good
sort, and most of us had grown quite fond of her - except those who
blamed her son for some of their afflictions. We buried her down by
the river - she liked it there. We all attended that day, someone said
a prayer, and we sang an old hymn - sort of seemed right somehow.
He just stood there and grinned. We all took it in turns to throw a
little earth on top of the coffin, but when someone took a shovel to
complete the job, the whole pile of earth just heaved itself up and fell
neatly into the grave. That's when we knew we were really in trouble.

Then we had a stroke of luck. One day, old Molly said we were
nearly out of lamp oil (We had been very careful of how we used it -
supplementing its use with homemade candles made from mutton fat
whenever possible - God, they were smelly).

The oil storage tank was very big, and we usually filled it once a year,
just before Christmas, and she had said, 'Wouldn't it be nice if the tank
was full again.' *He* must have been just within hearing of her remark -
next day the tank was full of oil.

One had to be very careful of how one wished, choosing one's words
with great care. Never, never ask directly - Frank did. 'I'd like some
nice fat chickens, real big 'uns.' He had said, with his usual toothless
grin. He got them alright. Next day he was overjoyed when he found
his yard full of chickens - and they were plump - no doubt about that.

Problem was, they kept putting on weight at a prodigious rate, and about two weeks later, most of them couldn't stand up - and none of them had laid a single egg. Poor old Frank - he was distraught, he kept standing them up, but they just fell over again - and then, one by one, they died as they couldn't feed themselves. *He* just stood around, laughing.

The wheat crop this year looked good - huge seed heads, golden brown, swaying gently in the soft breeze. We had just started harvesting it when a large black cloud came out of nowhere, and it began to rain. *He* was sitting on a rock at the edge of the field, grinning from ear to ear as we frantically tried to get the cut wheat under cover.

'Did you bring that cloud?' asked Dan, trying to hide what he really felt. *His* grin just got wider.

'Don't you realise that if we can't harvest this wheat, we'll all starve this coming winter? And then you'll be on your own,' said Dan, trying to smile at the same time. *He* just shrugged his shoulders, got up and walked away. We might go hungry, but he wouldn't - somehow he could spirit food away from anywhere - maybe even from out of our local town - *he* was always eating something, and we didn't always recognise it as being from our food stocks.

Dan was lucky - nothing seemed to happen to him, as far as we could tell. The rain cleared, and we got on with the harvesting, after waiting for the standing crop to dry out a little. Tempers were beginning to build up - we had been harassed by this little monster for ten years now, *he* seemed to get pleasure from seeing us suffer, and things were coming to a head.

We held a little meeting one evening in the disused barn at the edge of our hamlet - just the six of us. We knew we were safe from prying eyes, as *he* was entertaining himself decimating a flock of pigeons which had the misfortune to come into our area. *He* was making them crash into each other as they circled around, trying to find a perch for the night.

'I'd like to wring the little bastard's neck,' said Paul, his face flushed with anger. 'Given half a chance, I'd choke the bloody life out of him.'

We all knew this was impossible, because if we got close enough, *he* would just flit to one side - instantly - you didn't even see him move - one moment he was there, and the next several feet away.

A couple of years ago, Jan Mostec, who had been at the receiving end of his pranks for some time, had had enough. When his roof suddenly burst into flame for no apparent reason, and *he* was laughing his head off as Jan tried to throw water at it, Jan picked up a heavy piece of wood, and swung it at *his* head. It would have solved all our problems if it had landed, but it didn't. Just before contact, *he* flipped to one side, and Jan nearly fell over with the power of the swing. *His* laughter was gone, to be replaced with the ugliest contorted face I've ever seen - and Jan vanished. We searched all the buildings, the fields and woods, even waded into the river. We never did see him again.

'We've got to do something,' said Willy, 'we can't go on like this. We only just managed to harvest enough food to see us through the winter - remember last year? *He* did something to the potato clamp - they were all cooked when we opened it.'

We talked on into the evening, and when it got dark, we left to go our separate ways with nothing decided, except for Tim Riddler's idea. He suggested we dig a big pit with pointed stakes at the bottom, cover it up, and get *him* to chase us. *He* liked games, but what if *he* could stop himself from falling in? God knows what would happen to those *he* thought responsible.

At Christmas time, we all had to make *him* presents. If *he* didn't like one, the unfortunate person who made it usually brought up his Christmas dinner, or worse, couldn't keep food down for several days. We began to hate Christmas - it was so unpredictable. As *he* got older, he devised even more nasty surprises for us. We all went around with permanent smiles on our faces, saying how nice everything was, and what a nice person *he* was.

Poor old Violet Hepworthy, must have been eighty odd, dear old soul, kindness itself - never had a bad word for anyone. She did suffer from a lot of aches and pains, and a spot on her nose just wouldn't heal - it was forever oozing something unpleasant. One day she was hobbling over to the pump to get water when she tripped and fell - we couldn't see what she tripped over, it was just smooth ground. He was there of course. We helped her back up on her feet and she said, 'I wish I were dead, I can't stand this pain any more.' - and she dropped dead. *He* was grinning. We all turned and looked at him, and for the first time we saw fear on *his* face. He turned, and walked away - we saw little of *him* for the rest of the day, but on the morrow *he* was back to his usual obnoxious self, grinning or laughing at the little mishaps which befell us.

One day, two strangers came to our hamlet. They were taller than us, and were very strangely dressed - not unpleasantly so, but different.

We bade them the time of day, as one should, and they seemed very polite, asking how we were - we didn't dare tell them in case *he* overheard - but I could see they sensed something. They walked around the hamlet, looking into every cottage, and saying how nice and pretty they were - I think they were looking for something.

At last they came to the old forge, and seemed to tense up a little. One of them called out something I didn't understand, and a shadow at the back of the forge moved.

'Come out, it's no use trying to hide - we've found you,' said one of them, I think it was the man. Nothing happened, so he made an odd gesture with his hand and a shape came out from behind the bellows. It was *him* - but not as we knew him. *He* seemed to have shrunk, and walked awkwardly, as if he wasn't in full control of his legs.

'I think you have been very naughty,' said the man. 'Very naughty indeed.'

He hung his head, and the awful grin was gone.

'We don't know how you got away, but now we've found you - and you will come with us,' the man said firmly, grabbing him by the shoulder. The woman turned to me and said, 'I assume he was born here - what happened to his mother?'

I told her about the young woman, how she died, and that we had buried her by the river.

'You are a kind people, and we are very sorry you have been hurt so much. (How did she know that?) He will be punished severely for what he has put you through, we are only sorry we cannot undo what he has done.'

With that they left, with *him* between them, each with a hand firmly on each shoulder. Once they were out of sight, a cheer went up - they must have heard it - the terrible tension we had been under melted away - we were free at last.

The first thing we did, after a few good drinks of our beer, was to see if the mist was still there - it wasn't!

I hitched up my pony and trap, and raced off down the track to town, followed by several others - now we could buy all those things we had been missing for so long.

I wondered if we had come to the wrong place - a different town - it didn't look as it should. Once we had left the old track we were on a smooth black road - and the shops all looked different - brightly coloured, and containing goods we had never seen before. We got some funny looks from those people we passed, and they were dressed differently to us. The horses shied when a *horseless* carriage came rattling down the road towards us. What sort of world were we in? I stopped outside a shop which had some newspapers piled up on a box. I dismounted from the trap and picked up one of the papers - and looked at the date - *sixty years had passed since we had last been in town.*

A HUMAN AILMENT

THE ALIEN SHIP entered the solar system undetected, slipping in by masking itself behind the outer planets until it reached Mars - and then an astute observer at Mount Palomar noticed a slight distortion of the planet's image as it headed for Earth, and alerted other observatories.

By the time the huge ship had reached the moon's orbit, just about anyone with a decent telescope was looking for it, and the military were in deep discussion as to what they should do. At first, radio messages of welcome were sent in several languages and different frequencies, but there was no response from the dark shape except to go into orbit around the Earth, just outside the orbit of the International Space Station.

'Blast the Goddamn thing to hell - with fission tipped missiles,' was one suggestion from the military; while those of a more gentle nature, dressed in white flowing robes, assembled on the nearest high hill and chanted themselves hoarse with waving arms and copious amounts of cannabis.

By now, government heads were in deep consultation about the possible threat to Earth, although no hostile move had so far been taken by the alien ship. Several more attempts were made to communicate, using all known forms of data transmission, but there was no reply from the dark enigmatic shape.

There was some talk of sending up one of the Space Station's supply rockets with observers on board, but this was turned down as it might be taken for an act of aggression, and so the discussions went on with no decisions taken.

The real panic set in when the commutation satellites, one by one, suddenly failed after receiving a beamed pulse of electromagnetic radiation which fried their rather delicate internal workings. This left land-lines and the radio as the only way of communicating between nations, and that wouldn't last for long.

The military called up reservists, food stocks took a knocking from panic buying, and most churches did a roaring trade as extra prayer sessions were held. Several new religions sprang up overnight, purporting to be the only way to save humankind, and the Earth - but most required the giving up of all worldly goods and chattels, and large donations.

There were many reports of high voltage power lines burning out, followed by the power stations which supplied them - and then the panic really kicked in.

The military could no longer use their nuclear tipped rockets as their control systems and firing mechanisms relied on electrical power, and all but a few isolated generators had burnt out. Batteries were still functioning, so the price went up over- night - again and again, until stocks were exhausted - and now they couldn't be replenished.

Earth was just about defenceless, apart from hand guns and rifles, and those military weapons which didn't rely on electrical power. Radio stations had ceased to broadcast, as did television, and most telephones were out of action due to their overhead lines having burnt out. Aircraft were grounded, and all but a few ships managed to ply their trade, especially those equipped with sails.

Diesel engines (which didn't rely on electric pumps for their fuel) still functioned, but only while the fuel stocks lasted - and without electricity, no more fuel could be refined, although there were large stocks of crude oil.

Food stocks were hit as little transport still functioned, and it was 'grow your own' with a vengeance. Within weeks, there were hotspots of starvation as overcrowded cities could not get enough food in to supply the demand, and the population ventured out into the countryside to seek something to eat. The locals were not happy about this, as they too relied on imports to some extent, and what food they still had, they vigorously guarded with whatever came to hand. There were quite a few deaths as those 'who had' repelled those who 'had not'.

Most governments did their best to calm the situation, but with communications down, there was very little they could do.

And still the alien ship hung there, massive, black, and threatening, but so far no attempt had been made to physically invade the surface of Earth.

Slowly, a limited form of communication was established, using home made batteries and Morse code. These needed long aerials of wire to function, and as yet, the aliens hadn't burnt them out as they had done in the past.

Very slowly people got used to the reduced amount of food available, although many starved to death in the over crowded parts of the world. Armies were got ready, but there was nothing they could do except wave their weapons about and do lots of drill.

And then the flu hit. Type A influenza is unpleasant at the best of times, and these were not the best of times, by any means. Hospitals coped as best they could, but wards filled up very quickly, as did the corridors and store rooms - and then they ran out of beds. The elderly and weak suffered most. There was nothing anyone could do - except cough, sneeze, and wheeze, and for a moment the alien ship was forgotten by the general population.

Despite the normal method of infections spreading, air travel - of which there was none - the flu spread like wildfire, somehow leaping from continent to continent, but the congested cities were worst hit. When mankind was at its lowest ebb, the aliens decided to visit - personally.

Morse signals flashed around the world, stating that hoards of small ships were leaving the black monstrosity which had hung over Earth for so long. When the first ships landed, they were not as small as first thought, and the aliens must have been packed inside like sardines. Most chose to land near the big cities, which proved to be a big mistake in the long run.

They were quite human-like, but very stern looking - and not pretty. Any humans they encountered were herded into any large building which happened to be nearby, and speculation as to what would happen was rife - and not very pleasant.

The flu was at its peak, and with people feeling so ill and demoralised, they just obeyed the directions of the aliens - until the first annihilations began. Small metal canisters were thrown into crowded halls, and any space big enough to hold a few hundred people.

They weren't overtly cruel, just very efficient at what they were doing, clearing Earth of its human population.

It seemed painless, they just went to sleep, and then stopped breathing - but word got out - and spread via the Morse code system. Brute force was now needed to herd people to their doom.

Three days after the first landings and the subsequent massacres, the aliens began staggering about as if drunk, and lacked the usual eagerness to herd people into enclosed spaces. Wherever possible, their weapons were taken, and used against them - with an enthusiasm which had to be seen to be believed.

By the end of the second week, most of the aliens were dead, only those in remote places surviving, and then in a very wretched state. These were rounded up, and where possible, put into the high security prisons which were now almost empty of their old occupants (except for the corpses).

Once the main threat to life had passed, the power generators were rewound, and a skeletal grid system restored. Main telephone lines were replaced until the stocks of wire ran out, the rest of the system having to wait until wire production got under way again.

For some reason the aliens had switched off their equipment which burnt out most of Earth's power lines and damaged other electrical goods, such as the sparking systems in vehicle's engines, but these could be replaced until stocks ran out, and then it was a matter of 'repair where possible'.

Very slowly, life got back to near normal, or as normal as it would get with so much damage to the infrastructure. The population of Earth was now only about one third of what it had been before the invasion, but it now had some new technology to explore.

Those aliens who were now incarcerated were encouraged to help the engineers understand the workings of the transports from the black ship, which was still in orbit around Earth. Encouraged is perhaps a polite word for what actually took place - no holds were barred to obtain the necessary information.

It took a while, but eventually they learnt how to control the transports which brought the aliens to Earth, and a team took one of them up to the black ship. The size of the alien vessel was the greatest surprise; the second was that no one was on board - all the aliens had landed on Earth.

Although everyone cursed the flu when it came around every now and again, it had been Humanity's saviour - the aliens had no resistance to it, and it proved fatal to them.

THE PLANTING

WITH THE WORLD'S population exploding, especially in the poorer countries, well intentioned food aid was being dispatched in vast quantities to the starving millions.

This exacerbated the problem, as those who would have died from starvation were now able to grow up and have children of their own, meaning even more food would have to be produced and shipped. The ability to do this was nearing a critical point, as all the productive land that could be used was already under intensive cultivation, even attempts to farm the deserts had proved useless, as fresh water needed for irrigation was now in short supply as well.

Attempts at birth control made little difference to the problem, as some religions were against it, maintaining that 'God' would provide, and getting the message across to the uneducated masses was fraught with its own problems.

At a World Conference on food supply, the only two options left after lengthy discussions were, 'stop supplies' and 'go flat out for genetic modification of existing plants.' GM won the day, after many heated arguments and much fist waving.

The anti GM brigade then took up arms and went forth with all sorts of scare stories, and it was some time later before governments put their collective feet down, and gave the go ahead, insisting that extensive trials must be undertaken before the release of such food stuffs to the world in general.

Laboratories around the world set about the task of producing plants which were resistant to disease and which produced larger crops, but one team realised that even with success in this field, the problem would never be solved - man reproduced too prolifically. So they went down a different route.

They decided to build a new type of plant, using existing plant material, but engineered to produce something which was totally usable - stems, leaves and fruit.

Three years later, and with the food situation getting even worse, they came up with the first trials. Of all the mutations they had produced, one seemed to be a clear winner.

It was not unlike a tomato plant, except that it grew to a full three metres in height and produced large leaves which tasted much like a sweet cabbage. It produced large quantities of a brown pear shaped fruit, rich in minerals and vitamins, and with a pleasant flavour like no other. The stems were a bit fibrous and tough, but when dried and milled, made a very palatable food for herbivores - in fact they seemed to prefer it to grass in tests which were done. It was a little later when they found that the roots, if dried and ground, made a beverage not unlike coffee, but with a slight liquorice flavour. All in all, there was very little wastage, and the team were given the go ahead to produce commercial quantities of the plant to distribute to growers around the world.

Even in countries which had poor soil and little natural water, the new plants seemed to thrive, growing a little slower perhaps, but still producing plentiful food.

Some insects seemed to enjoy nibbling at the leaves, but somehow the plant managed to seal off the chewed edges of its leaves, and they continued to grow unharmed.

Someone decided to see if the plants would grow even taller if given a support, and that produced an unexpected effect. Once the plant had reached four metres in height, it sprouted another set of flowers, but they didn't produce fruit. Small seed pods formed as the flowers withered and died, and these duly ripened and burst, releasing seeds with a fluffy tuft at one end, not unlike a dandelion seed.

No one gave much thought to this unexpected phenomenon, until someone noticed that the seeds were viable, and young plants had sprung up some months later. Within a year, this self seeding was being reported from all around the world, but no one seemed to mind, as the labour intensive job of planting out seedlings was now reduced, and would soon become redundant.

At long last, the world's food problems seemed to have been solved, but another was now rearing its ugly head. In the near future, there would not be enough land to live on and grow food. The cities had all expanded, reaching out into the countryside to an alarming extent, and if something wasn't done, overcrowding would be the next problem.

Another strange trait of the new food source was that when it grew over four metres, and there was enough wind to threaten the plants, they sent out side shoots which when they touched a nearby plant, seemed to meld into it, thus forming a solid self supporting mass - and then the plants put on another couple of metres in growth.

Where the fluffy seeds had landed, other plants were stunted, or refused to grow altogether. Even some trees had died, and when examined, it was thought the new plants were releasing some sort of toxin, preventing anything else from growing in close proximity to them.

As the minerals and other nutrients in the top soil were used up, the roots were driven down to unprecedented depths, no normal plant on Earth could extend its roots this far, and some began to wonder if they had released an uncontrollable monster.

On one plantation near the sea, someone noticed that the plants had spread across the beach, and were now forming a thin mat on the actual water - somehow they had developed a salt tolerance. The leaves were a darker green, and the fruits not so prolific, but the plants were thriving. Sometime later, a fisherman noticed that fish were feasting on this new bonanza of food, and the inshore shoals of fish were growing steadily.

At long last, the message got through - keep your families small, or you'll have nowhere to live. It had taken a long time, and a lot of unnecessary suffering for the fact to be accepted by most of the world's population, but the growth rate steadied out.

A frightening report came in from Africa - large areas of what was once a vast forested area was now covered in the new plants, replacing the original trees, and was now spreading out onto the open plains. A similar report came in from the Amazon and other South American states - even the huge grass prairies were shrinking.

Although everyone had plenty to eat, concern was now growing that the plants were now out of control, so herbicides were tried to slow things down a bit - but the plants had been engineered to be resistant to just about anything, and were proving the point. Huge mats of the marine variety were now spreading out for several kilometres across the ocean, and choking small harbours, despite the locals hacking it back.

Just about all marine animals were enjoying the new food supply, and were multiplying accordingly, but getting out to catch them was becoming a problem - except for the large commercial harbours, which were equipped with cutting and trawling machines, and they were having to go flat out to keep the waterways open.

From space, Earth had taken on a new green mantle not seen for thousands of years, but it was a uniform green covering, lacking the variety of times gone by.

The new vast forests which now covered the Earth were reducing the carbon dioxide in the atmosphere, and the strange effect of this was to increase rainfall - and that gave the plants a boost. Panic set in when it was noticed that in some places the plants had encroached into the built up areas, and were now invading actual buildings, sending shoots into every nook and cranny, seeking out nutriments wherever they were to be found. Concrete seemed to be favoured to brick, so far, but even brick had been attacked according to some reports.

For the first time in thousands of years, the World's population was beginning to fall as the people were being squeezed into smaller and smaller spaces. It was a continuous struggle to cut the plants back to obtain a living space - steel being the only thing which seemed immune to the attack of the green monster, and now there was a limit on how much of that was available, as mining was almost impossible due to the choking effect the plants had on the transport system.

The anti GM advocates had a field day, but most people were more concerned about everyday living to pay much attention. There was plenty to eat, but not much free space to eat it in.

Some of the larger plants, mainly in the big forests, had mutated yet again, and seemed more like the trees of old. They were difficult to get to, but great efforts were made to do so as normal wood was just about unobtainable now. Felling and extraction was difficult, but it was done as the demand for timber soared.

A few years on, and from the air, most cities looked like huge green mounds - some people did live in them, but it wasn't an easy life. Research and science fell by the wayside, as what was left of the population sought a more simple form of life. Some built colonies on the huge floating mats of vegetation which fringed all the land masses, fishing for food as the marine growth produced little in the way of fruit.

Others abandoned the overgrown cities, and sought refuge in the more tree-like parts of the forests. They seemed to prefer to keep in small groups, but were in touch with other groups around, the mighty branches being the highways on which they travelled.

The original food plants had mutated into something like the trees of old Earth, but they were much bigger by several orders of magnitude - and joined together to form, in effect, one giant growing mass. Other plants and vines grew on the mighty trees, producing fruits and nuts to sustain the little groups of humans, but now the animals which had survived also changed to suit the levels in which they lived. They were, over time, many and varied. Not all ate fruit, and many humans provided an unintentional meal until they learned to avoid or overcome them.

And so life had been brought back into balance. Man had nearly ruined Earth, but by his own hand, unknowingly, had restored a new and vibrant balance to nature.

As time passed, newer species of plant and animal life came about, driven not only by the huge change in the environment - but also by the original plant gene manipulation, which, because it had been consumed, transferred its gene changing properties to all who had eaten it.

These new creations found their place in which to live in the vast forests, some up in the tree tops, others a little lower down, and an assortment of crawling and wriggling things inhabited the forest floor, where it was almost dark; their main food source being those creatures who lived above who had died or been injured, and fallen to the depths below.

Once more, Earth was in balance - but for how long would that last?

MOVING ON

I DON'T KNOW exactly how old I am, I have no recollection of childhood - I just seem to be. My earliest memories are of the Egyptian times, about the time of the pyramids. I actually helped build them. One thing I have learned is that you can't always trust written history. As far as I can recall, they weren't built using slaves - quite the opposite - we were well fed and looked after, and even paid for our labours.

There is no way they could have controlled that many slaves on such a massive project, and over so much time. We were all willing builders, although the purpose of the construction was not understood by many.

As with all great civilisations, complacency and decadence brought about their fall, which was a shame really - they seemed to have it all together at one time.

The Minoans, although that isn't what they called themselves, were the wealthiest traders in their area, and built up a great civilisation, but their end came with the island of Thera blowing itself up, and totally destroying their trading along with the crops and most of their infrastructure. I do not recall a greater volcanic eruption since that sad time. They turned to barbarism in their confusion, not understanding why they had been smitten, and that was the end of them. Later, the early Greeks invaded to complete the job.

All through my life, and it's been a very long one, I have moved from one developing civilisation to the next, my body and skin colour seemingly changing to suit whatever race I join. I have had my fair share of accidents, but always seem to recover from them at an amazing rate, and over time I have come to accept this, along with many other strange things which happen to me. I am never short of currency, always acquiring enough for my needs with little effort.

But there is one thing I don't like; I can't keep a relationship for long as I don't seem to age, and sooner or later awkward questions are asked. It isn't to say I haven't fathered many children - I have, hundreds of them over time, but I never see them grow up. It is quite heartbreaking really, I build up a relationship, but after a while, I have to find a way to end it - always as painlessly as possible - but end it I must. Something inside me drives me to do this, and I often wish it didn't.

Another strange thing is the dreams. Every few years, I dream someone is asking me to recall all I have witnessed, in great detail -

especially anything scientific, like metal working or medicine. And then I am told, *'you may return'* and the dream ends. The odd thing is that the person asking the questions seems to change every couple of hundred years - can't see much of them though, just the head and shoulders.

I do realise I am not like others, aging and dying; and I can't explain it, nor can those few people I have talked to about it - I don't think they believed me.

After the Egyptian civilisation collapsed, I felt the urge to move north into what is now called Europe. I don't understand why, as they were really barbaric, and the quality of life was well below that which I had enjoyed so far. In time, things got a little better as metallurgy improved and new inventions came about. The old alchemy gave way to chemistry proper, and then things improved immensely.

When the first flying machines took to the air, the dreams asking for details of man's progress became more frequent and intense - in a way I felt I was betraying the people I lived among, but these were only dreams, and no one else could hear or see what was in them.

There had been many wars before, but when the Great War took place I began to worry that man would destroy himself - and the Second World War convinced me of this, but there was little I could do about it. The dreams came every few months now, and I began to hate them. I felt drained after having one, and it took several days before I felt my old self again.

It was getting more difficult now to remain anonymous; everyone seemed to have an identity kept on record somewhere, and I had to keep changing my place in society more frequently.

When the first atomic bomb was dropped, the person in my dreams got very persistent about the details, and I had to go to the USA. I didn't want to, but the urge to do so was overwhelming. How I got into the research plant, I don't know, but I got a job there somehow. I seemed to be able to move around at will - no one tried to stop me, and that seemed a bit strange as they seemed very security conscious. The dreams were every few weeks now, and I tried to ask why this was so, but in the dream my questions weren't answered - the questioner just smiled - and the dream ended.

The first men to the moon and the communication satellites seemed to get the person in my dreams somewhat agitated, as the questions became more probing in their detail, and very persistent. The main interest seemed to be about man's ability to go into space -

the Explorer range of probes, and those which followed seemed to be of little interest, but man himself getting into space seemed to cause some consternation.

My dreams became even more frequent after I mentioned the building of the space station. A new person has come into my dreams - stern faced and almost aggressive in his questioning - I didn't like him, but I couldn't stop the dreams.

One night I asked him why he was so upset about the space station, he just said,

'*You just do your job, that's what you're there for.*' He somehow looked as if he wished he hadn't said that - and I began to wonder about myself and the dreams. I was different to all the others on this world, and the dreams didn't seem like dreams now - more like someone reporting back to somewhere, but I've no idea where.

Several weeks went by before the next dream, and it was someone else who was there. He seemed a much nicer person, smiling a lot, and with a gentle voice.

After the usual questions, I asked him if he could tell me about myself, as I wasn't like the others here. He paused for a moment, and said, '*I will try and get permission to do that.*' And the dream ended.

It was getting very difficult to get a job anywhere, let alone in the space project. Everyone else had an identity, a record of who they were - I had nothing - I appeared on no records (as far as I know) - I was a non-person - I didn't exist; life was getting very difficult indeed trying to remain undetected, and I somehow knew I must.

The next time I had a dream, after I had answered as best as I could all the questions, I asked if I could ask some. There was a pause, and then it was agreed I could. I wanted to know who I was exactly, and why I was here on this world.

'How come I don't die like all the other people when they get old or ill?' A pause.

'*It has been decided to tell you about yourself, and the work you do for us because it is almost done now. You don't die because your genes have been altered - you may not fully understand this, but the telomeres on your chromosomes have been altered so that they do not decrease in length as they do in other humans. Also your immune system has been altered to cope with any infection you may pick up. This means you will never age, and you will heal from any accident very quickly.*

There are many worlds with civilisations on them, and when they are discovered, we put someone on them to monitor their technical progress.

If, when they reach the stage of space flight and are considered suitable, they are invited to join the Confederation for trade and exchange of technical data - if they show signs of instability or aggression, they have to be excluded for the good of all other members.

Unfortunately, the people of your world have advanced technically to a high degree, but mentally and emotionally they are far behind that which is required to join the Confederation, and so will be excluded until they meet our requirements. This means that they will not be able to leave their solar system. They will be free to explore anywhere within the system, but interstellar space will be barred to them. How we do this, you don't need to know, nor would you understand the technical aspect of it, as your science has not advanced enough to grasp the concept.

With regards to yourself, we can tell you how to terminate your life should you wish to do so, or you can carry on as you are - you will not age, so you might find it interesting to see how your people advance - or not. You will not have many more dreams, as we have all the data we need. You may dream occasionally as we would be interested in your progress - but it will be infrequent. Is there anything else you would like to know?'

'Yes, where is my real home world - where did I come from?'

'You came from where you are now. We picked up a body which looked suitable, altered it to suit our needs, and sent it back - I think it was in what you refer to as the early Egyptian period. You really do belong to your world - you just have some abilities not shared by others. Anything else?'

I paused for a while, trying to gather up my thoughts and any other questions - but then the dream ended.

This had put a whole new light on my life, and I am interested to see how man will progress. First I must obtain an identity. I have heard such things can be bought, if one has enough money - and somehow, money does not to seem to be a problem for me.

If you see a good looking young man, in the peak of health, who does not age as you do, we may have met.

THE STEPS

I ENJOY EXPLORING old buildings - really old ones. Done the Pyramids - spent nearly a month there (even bought a rather dodgy tee shirt - colours ran on the first wash).

I was looking through an old book one day which described a very ancient monastery up north somewhere, so thought I'd give it a try - that's if I could find it.

It took nearly a week to locate the place, and then it was almost by chance. I was sitting in this very old pub in a little village at the back of beyond, supping some of their local ale, when someone mentioned the tower.

'What's that?' I asked. 'Anything to do with the old monastery?'

'You don't want to go there,' this old boy said, 'the place is evil - no good ever come of going up there. When I was a lad, young Icky went up there - they said he went into it, but no one knows for sure - anyway, us never saw Icky again, and after that they put a padlock on the door.'

'Where is it?' I asked, hopefully. But there was no reply, and shortly afterwards the old boy left, with his drinking partner.

I booked a room for a couple of nights, and asked the landlord about the old monastery, but he wasn't having any of it either.

Next day, I stopped a young lad in the village, and asked him. He didn't seem worried about it, and gave clear directions, although he said he had never been up there himself. Mentioned something about there being some four hundred and twenty steps to the top, but he wasn't sure.

'Do you know of anyone who's ever been up there?' I asked, hoping to get more information.

'No, my dad said 'twas a dangerous place, what with all them old walls crumbling down, so none of us goes there.'

Now I had directions, it was just a matter of finding the place - but I was surprised just how difficult that was. I followed the old cart track, as directed, and then that petered out, so it was a matter of tramping across the moor, in what I hoped was the correct direction. After about an hour, I could see a tall structure on the horizon, and as I drew nearer, the old monastery building came into sight.

I stopped for my packed lunch once I had reached the actual ruins, sitting down in what I assumed to be the nave. It was very old, only the main walls remaining partially intact, but the bell tower still stood solid and firm. The doorway into the tower was blocked with fallen rubble, so I could not get in - pity really, as it would have given a wonderful view across the moor.

After exploring the ruins and making notes of anything interesting, I decided to explore the main tower, which stood only some twenty metres away.

On close inspection, the tower was a good deal older than the monastery, judging by the stonework, and sure enough, the door at the base was padlocked. There being no other way in, I decided to see if I could pick the lock, but it too was very old, and rusted solid. I had come all this way, and now I was stopped by a locked door - as no one ever came up here, would it matter if I removed the lock? I didn't think so.

A couple of blows with a hefty piece of rock shattered the old lock, and I now had access. It was dark and dank smelling, but old places usually are, so that didn't put me off. The floor inside the tower was flagged with huge pieces of stone, carefully fitted together with hardly a crack between them, and the steps, although well worn, seemed solid enough. I pulled the old wooden door closed behind me so that my eyes would get used to what little light came in through the narrow slits in the walls above.

And now the great climb could begin. With my knapsack on my back, I put a foot onto the first step, and decided to count the steps as I went up - at least I could check the total number to see if it was correct.

I had to stop half way up - I was exhausted, and took some sustenance from my knapsack along with a drink - I certainly could have done with one of those beers from last night. After resting for a while, I was about to resume the climb when I heard a bell tolling - it was very distant, and had a strange hollow sound. I hadn't noticed a church in the little village the day before, in fact I'm sure there wasn't one - so where was the bell chime coming from?

I continued to climb, wishing in a way that I hadn't started in the first place. Up ahead it seemed a little lighter, I must be near the top. And then I was out in brilliant sunlight. The number of steps was exactly as the boy had said, four hundred and twenty. The view from the top was amazing, rolling countryside going off into the hazy distance. I thought I should have seen the village from this height, but there was no sign of it - or of any other buildings.

I turned around, and there was the monastery, in all it's glory - I could even see some monks wandering around. And then the monastery bell began to toll, I could see it swing to and fro in the top of the monastery tower, and all the monks scurried into the main building - but it was different to the bell I had heard in my tower. A few minutes later and the chanting began - but it seemed to be echoing in the old tower I was standing in - welling up from below. The hairs on the back of my neck stood up - something was wrong here. Had I somehow been sent back in time? That was impossible, but the monastery was now whole, complete with monks too.

It was too much - I wanted out of here. With one more quick look around, I began the descent, counting the steps again - I don't know why - I just did. Still I could hear the monks chanting - from below. It seemed like a tinny recording played back in a large echo chamber - unnerving to say the least.

At four hundred and twenty I looked for the door - it wasn't there - the steps just went on down. Had I miss counted? I continued on down, there was no alternative, but now it was getting darker. I took my windup torch from the knapsack, gave it a few turns and carried on. At five hundred I stopped. Something was seriously wrong - I couldn't have made that much of a mistake.

I was now bathed in a cold sweat, and shaking. The steps still went on down into the darkness below, and there was no light from the tiny slits in the wall. Perhaps it was nightfall, or a cloud had covered the sun.

Only one thing for it, go back up again. There was no sign of the old wooden door on the way up, and I checked thoroughly. I was shattered by the time I reached the top of the tower, and it was night time. There was no moon, but the stars were sharp and bright - a few lights shone from the monastery, but even as I watched, they went out, one by one.

In desperation, I wrote down what had happened - begging for help, and then tying the bundle of papers up with some string, threw it out from the top of the tower. Perhaps someone would find it and come to my rescue. I ate the last of the food, and settled down for a long wait...

EXCHANGELING

I KNEW I had been ill for some time, but I wouldn't confront it. In the past, I think the doctors were getting fed up with my frequent visits - they couldn't seem to find anything wrong which made any sense. After a long period of pills and lotions, probes and scans, I gave up - much to their relief, I suspect.

But things had now taken a turn for the worst; I lacked the energy to do the everyday things most of us do without thinking, even a short walk drained me for several hours afterwards - I had aches and pains all over, and nothing seemed to work properly anymore. I had even given up my water colour painting - something I was quite good at, even sold a few; and the piano really was a thing of the past - it made my fingers and arms ache.

I made one last attempt to sort things out - found a new young doctor who didn't like to be beaten - went through a whole load of tests, and he diagnosed all my major organs were failing, mainly due to a faulty heart valve.

The date was set for the valve to be sorted out, and I went under the anaesthetic with some trepidation - had a bad feeling about it, but I would soon shuffle off this mortal coil if nothing was done.

The lights faded, and I seemed to be in limbo - but I knew I was still me, and that sounds odd, I know.

And then I could see; I was floating above my body on the operating table, while two surgeons plus several others leaned over my open chest, and seemed to be in a state of panic. Someone wheeled up a trolley with a machine on it - two flat plates were placed on my chest, and all but one stepped back - my body gave an almighty jerk - again, and again, and then they took the machine away. Must admit, they did look disappointed. A sheet was drawn up over my body's head, and they left.

But I was still me; I could see, and then I could hear a little. I found life in the hospital quite fascinating - always something new going on day and night - must say I did miss my body - but I was still me. That got me to thinking; what was I? - the *real* me? I was aware - could think - had a memory, but no body. Perhaps I was the real driving force in the body - the thing which made it move and do things - that seemed reasonable. Perhaps I was what they call the 'soul'. But people say you *have* a soul - they got that wrong! You don't *have* one - you *are* one!

Imagine a car driving along - it stops - the driver gets out, but he leaves the engine running. The driver is the controller, the soul or spirit. The car is the body - the engine will keep running (until the fuel runs out), but the driver isn't in it - it needs the driver to complete the whole unit - yes, it makes a lot of sense, to me anyway.

Watching someone take a hot chocolate drink from the machine reminded me that I missed that side of life. I didn't feel hungry or thirsty, but I could remember what it felt like to indulge in such things. I was not a little surprised about what some of the nurses and doctors got up to - after all, we're all human - well they are.

I don't remember how long I hung around that hospital - time doesn't seem to mean much now, but I think it was quite a while. I was beginning to miss the interaction with the physical world - I know I can do things I couldn't do before my body died, but contact with the real world has its own joys - and I was beginning to miss them - very much.

I was in A&E one day, when a body was wheeled in - two doctors gave it a quick check over, and it was sent up to intensive care at great speed. I followed to see what they would do. There had been some damage to it which they cleaned up, and then a series of tubes were inserted, and it was wired up to a monitor.

Some time later, a man and a woman came in to sit by the body - one held its hand, and both were crying softly. I felt sorry for them, but there was nothing I could do. The days passed, and their visits became less frequent - I think the stress was too much for them to take.

I heard a man in a dark blue suit say that the coma was very deep, and he didn't think the person would ever recover, as there was no brain activity - the body was brain dead. There was some talk of removing the life support system, but permission would have to be gained first.

I moved very close to the body, and somehow sensed that whoever had been in it, was now gone - it was an empty shell, all the life force had gone, and it was only the machines which gave the semblance of life.

It was male, as I am, and I wondered if I dared try and take it on - would it be possible? It seemed ethical enough, the person who had it didn't seem to need it any more, and physically it looked in good condition, as all the damage had been repaired.

I got as close to the body as possible, but nothing happened - and then I remembered the feeling of the hot chocolate…….and snap - I was surrounded by warm flesh.

I tried to open my eyes, but they were stuck shut; by forcing the muscles, it made my eyes water, and first one opened, and then the other - I could see. I tried to move my arms and legs, but they seemed lifeless, although I could feel them - I knew where they were.

A short while later a nurse came in to check the instruments, and having done so she looked me straight in the face - My eyes were open, so I blinked. 'Oh,' and she left the room in a great hurry. A few moments later, and she returned with a doctor.

'Can you hear me?' he said. 'Blink if you can.'

I blinked furiously. He turned to the nurse, 'This sometimes happens, but not very often. Bathe his eyes, and I'll get Mr. Johnson.'

Over the next few days I got more control over my new body - I could now waggle my fingers, turn my head a little, but the body still felt very weak. The tubes and other attachments were gradually withdrawn, except the feeding tube, but I was unable to speak - I managed a few grunts, but that was all.

I heard someone say, 'We'll let him recover a little more and stabilise before we tell the parents, we don't want to give them a double shock if things go wrong.'

Gradually I gained control over this new body, but it wasn't easy. I could now raise my arms a little, move my legs, and utter a few words - but I found it exhausting.

A day or so later, and two nurses helped me out of bed. I felt a bit wobbly on my feet, but I could move them, and with their help, was able to walk a few steps.

'We are going to tell your parents of your recovery, would you like that?'

I had been dreading this moment - I didn't know them, or anything about them, and they would expect me to. I would have to dramatise memory loss - couldn't think of any other way around the problem.

'Yes please, but explain to them that I have lost my memory, can't remember a thing about them.'

The following day my 'parents' came in; they were overjoyed, with tears glistening in their eyes. I felt sad that I couldn't greet them as their son, but I had to keep up the pretence, otherwise I'd be in all sorts of trouble - and if they found out the truth - I dread to think what the outcome of that would be, they had been hurt enough.

It was explained to them that it would be some little time before I could be taken home, as my musculature had to be built up, and I was unable to take solid food.

And so the long haul to recovery began. The feeding tube came out a few days later, and I tried solid food - well, actually it was a bowl of mush, but it tasted good. The rebuilding of my muscles took a bit longer, the exercising was agony, but it had to be done.

One day, Mr Johnson came to see me, in his smart pinstripe suit. He was a very stern man, but seemed to know his job.

'I wonder if you can explain how you claim to have lost all your memory of the past, but know what words mean, and can speak fluently.'

'I don't know either, Mr. Johnson, it's got me puzzled too. I just remember waking up, and after a lot of effort, opened my eyes - and you know the rest.'

'Hmmm.' Was all he said to that, turned to the nurses and said, 'He can go home tomorrow, his parents will fetch him if you tell them.'

Next morning the car turned up, complete with excited parents. At least I was ambulant, and able to experience the physical world again. You have no idea how good hospital custard tastes after a long absence.

They were waiting for me at reception, and after the hugs and kisses, it was into the car and we sped away to a new life - for them and me.

It was a nice house in a nice area, all the lawns were clipped short, the flower borders bloomed - all in all, it looked very nice indeed.

The parents, Bob and Sue, were very sympathetic and understanding, not asking too much of me, and letting me set the pace, as it were. I still rested a lot, but I was growing stronger day by day.

Funny, I hadn't noticed the piano in the corner of the lounge before - but I had now. Without thinking, I sat down and ran my fingers over the keys - it felt good to play again. Soon I was belting out all the old favourites - and then the parents came in.

'I had no idea you could play,' Father said, incredulously, 'You always hated the piano. You only had two lessons, and then refused to go again. Where on earth did you learn to play like that?'

'I don't know - it just came to me,' I lied. 'It must have been that bang on the head, I suppose, I wonder what else I can do?'

They sat down and asked me to play on, which I did, but it had shaken them somewhat. I would have to be very careful in the future. They seemed to be enjoying the music, so I carried on, until my hands ached.

I decided to do some research, and found there had been several accounts of people coming out of a coma with totally different personalities - and no one could explain it. Perhaps we believe verbatim the dogma of some religions, never querying it - and the significance of the brain, it certainly doesn't fit in with what has happened to me.

A few days later, as I was walking down the street to the shops, a young lady called out to me.

'I heard you were home and well - that's wonderful, we all missed you. Will you be coming down to the club?'

'Not just yet,' I replied. 'I'm sorry, I don't think I know you.'

'Oh, I forgot,' she replied, 'they said you had lost your memory - I'd forgotten, sorry. We'll have to see what we can do to remedy that - you'll be in for a few surprises.' And with that, she bounced off down the road, swinging her hips provocatively.

This wasn't going to be as easy as I had thought. What other relationships had been built which I didn't know about? The easy way out would be to just leave and start a new life somewhere else, but I couldn't hurt the 'parents' - they had got their boy back, against huge odds, and seemed so happy now.

After a couple of months, I had settled in quite well - made a few friends, although some down at the club eyed me with suspicion for a while. Found it a bit difficult calling the parents Mum and Dad, but got used to it in time.

Just had a thought - if I, as a free spirit could take on a body which had been abandoned, what's to stop me taking on a new born baby at the moment of birth? - That would make me immortal! You know, the fear of death has completely gone!

Have to wait until this body packs up before I can try it…

THE RETURN

THE ONLY WAY we could explore the other planets in our solar system was a drive unit capable of that approaching the speed of light - and that seemed impossible -until now. The theory looked alright, so a scale model was constructed, luckily not big enough to sit in.

We all waited anxiously as the countdown crawled down to zero - and the bloody thing just disappeared - with a bit of a bang as the air readjusted itself.

'Good thing nobody was in it,' someone commented. 'With that acceleration, they'd just be a strawberry jam smear on the rear bulkhead.'

The theory boys said this wouldn't happen, as the field set up by the drive unit encompassed the whole craft, and anything in it - but it was only theory.

Another craft was assembled with control electronics, such that it would go forward for three seconds, turn around, and then go forward again for the same amount of time - the idea being it should return to its starting place. And just to placate the doubters, a small compartment was constructed to hold a mouse. 'Animal Rights' were up in arms when they found out our intentions - so they were invited to take the mouse's place. Needless to say, there were no takers on that idea, and they faded away into the shrubbery.

After another three weeks, launch day arrived. Benny (named after our project director) was ensconced in his little capsule, and the countdown hit zero. The craft seemed to shimmer for a split second - and there it was, pointing in the opposite direction to what it had been - this time the bang was a bit bigger. The craft itself was a bit warm, but Benny was just fine.

Next, a craft was built big enough to take a man - but volunteers were a bit thin on the ground, not surprising really. Finally, money solved the problem, and we had our pilot - not that he would have to do much piloting, as it had been decided to use electronics to control the whole operation.

A couple of months later, and we were ready to test the contraption. The pilot climbed into his compartment - looking a bit sick - perhaps it was the light.

The idea was to do a ten second test run, and return. It worked just fine, but the craft was just short of glowing due to the friction of going through the Earth's atmosphere at such speed. Can't think why no one had thought about the friction - the poor pilot was a deep pink when he climbed out, and sweating and swearing profusely. At this time it was realised that the noise from the ruptured air was going to be a problem, as several scientists shook their heads, trying to get their hearing back.

Anyway, it worked. Now construction of a full size vehicle could go ahead, and this time there were no shortage of volunteers for the trip. During construction, someone had figured out a way of controlling the speed, and tried it out on a smaller vehicle - that did away with the huge sonic boom the full size craft would have made.

It took nearly a year to complete the craft, with everyone working flat out. She would carry a crew of six, with two landing craft to explore anything which looked remotely stable to land on. By now, the volunteers were fighting among themselves for a place on the 'Lightrace' as she was going to be called, including two who thought they would be able to contact God, once clear of the Earth's atmosphere.

The great day came, and we all climbed aboard amid much cheering and clapping of hands. To be honest, I was a bit apprehensive, but all the tests had been done, and no problems found - or if there were, no one had told us.

Liftoff was smooth and silent, apart from a rushing noise as we cleaved our way out of the atmosphere and into space. The space station looked magnificent as we passed it, gleaming in the bright light of the sun, a huge jumble of spars and modules with their solar cells sparkling. I wondered if we really needed it now.

It had been decided that we would visit Mars first - just a quick look, and then out into deep space towards the great gas giant planets.

It was a strange feeling, travelling at such huge velocities, but it meant we could now explore the rest of the solar system, and then perhaps, intergalactic space.

Mars was much like all the pictures we had seen of it - red, barren, but the surface had some interesting features, especially the poles; it was still not known for sure if the white polar caps were snow or frozen carbon dioxide.

We did a few manoeuvres, and then the navigator announced that we had a clear run right out to the edge of our solar system. We didn't think Pluto was worth a visit, as it was only about the size of Mercury, and according to reports, was just a frozen lump of rock; Neptune was our first goal, being the outermost planet of our system.

The command was given, and the ship accelerated with hardly any sense of motion - still couldn't get used to that idea - didn't seem right somehow, but this was a new technology, and it had been explained to us that the whole ship was enclosed in the field which drove the ship, and therefore we wouldn't feel anything.

Oh, one other thing. The original test craft had to turn through one hundred and eighty degrees to come back to where it started from - and this could be problematic on the full scale ship, so they found a way of reversing the drive field so that we could decelerate without having to turn around.

I was surprised how fast we had travelled, as deceleration took place as we were having a meal break. Neptune, in all its glory came into sight in the forward viewing port. A beautiful blue, with signs of swirling clouds of gas in its outer layer. It's about seventeen times the mass of Earth, but not quite as dense. The atmosphere, according to our instruments, is mainly hydrogen and helium, with traces of methane - the methane giving it the lovely blue colour. As far as we can tell, the core of the planet is mainly composed of ice and rock - iron, nickel and silicates. Again according to our instruments, the core is about five thousand degrees Kelvin, while the outer atmosphere is down to fifty five degrees Kelvin - which is about as cold as you can get and still have a gaseous atmosphere.

There is no way we could land on Neptune, so after taking all the reading we could, we set off for Neptune's largest moon, Triton. It appears to be a rocky frozen lump, and somehow doesn't seem to belong to Neptune, because of its structure, and it has a retrograde orbit, which would indicate that it originated somewhere else, and was captured by Neptune's massive gravity field. There were many more smaller moons around Neptune, but apart from noting their position and possible composition, we left for Uranus.

Although Uranus appears larger than Neptune, it is not so dense, and doesn't radiate so much heat. It is blue tending to green, due to a similar composition to Neptune, and about fourteen times the mass of Earth. Again, we can't land on it as it's a 'gas giant' with no solid surface. We checked the moons for anything interesting, but they were mostly composed of rock and ice, and not really worth a visit.

And so on to Saturn, possibly the most interesting planet in the outer reaches of the solar system. As we approached, the rings showed up better than any photograph taken by Explorer. There were many small 'moons', most just lumps of rock, but Titan is the biggest, and with an atmosphere - but not like Earth's. Some of the gasses detected would suggest that some form of very primitive life might exist on its surface, but it was not possible to view the surface due to the orange haze which surrounded the moon, and therefore a safe landing could not be made -tempted as we were. One puzzling thing we noticed was that the atmosphere appeared to rotate faster than the moon itself.

Jupiter was the next planet to be visited - it is massive, by far the biggest of all the planets in the solar system. Again it is a 'gas giant', mainly composed of hydrogen and about ten to twelve per cent helium, appearing to be striped in blue and a pale muddy brown. Below the atmosphere is liquid metallic hydrogen, a strange substance - of which little is known. There were many moons, some sixty six in all, but only four were worthy of exploration.

Io, an orange colour, was so far the most colourful moon we had seen, but the volcanic activity on its surface precluded any attempt to land. It is thought Io gets its internal heat from the high gravitational forces of Jupiter, as it is in close orbit around the planet, plus an interaction with the other moons.

Europa was the next moon to visit. Our instruments indicated it was mostly composed of silica in the form of rock, but it had an atmosphere of oxygen. The smooth surface with little sign of cratering, suggested the surface might be fluid, or formed of ice. The ship went into orbit, and a Lander was prepared to take two of us down to the surface. I would go with Ben, our engineer, as he was used to operating the ground penetrating radar. From the ship, we had determined that the surface ice (if it was ice) was very thick - far too thick for our radar to penetrate, so we would look for an area where there had been a recent eruption of the surface, hoping it might be a little thinner there. What convinced us of water being present was the fact that the density of the lower layer was higher than that above. (Water ice having a lower density).

It was the first time I had piloted the Lander in real time - although the simulator on Earth gave a pretty good approximation of what it would be like. We slipped away from the ship and cruised along the surface of the moon at about five hundred metres, looking for recent surface activity.

What had appeared smooth from the ship proved to be nothing like what we saw now. The surface was ruptured, with huge plates of ice piled up upon one another; deep rifts, many hundred of metres deep, and deep pits many thousands of metres across. It was some time before we saw what we wanted - newly broken ice in a deep depression. The Lander gently touched down, and suited up, we unloaded the radar unit and set it up.

The ice here was relatively thin, compared to that which surrounded us, but even so, it would push the radar unit to its limits. Ben set up the recording machine, so that the data could be analysed more fully when back on the ship, and the first pulses of energy were sent down through the ice.

We could just make out moving shapes beneath, but it was difficult to gauge their size - that would be done back on the ship, later. Some were long and thin, others more whale-like - but what convinced us that they were alive was their ability to change direction as they swam below us. The readout pictures were a bit hazy, but there was no doubt that something was moving about down there. The outside microphones picked up a couple of sharp cracks, and the ice beneath our feet trembled - it was time to leave. Back in the ship, the data was analysed, and the swimming shapes took on a new clarity - yes, there was life down there, but there was no way we could get at it.

Ganymede and Calisto are similar in make up and appearance, both heavily pitted with impact craters, and we decided at this point to return to Earth, leaving the last two moons to be explored by someone else.

For some inexplicable reason, I was beginning to feel nervous - not about the ship, it had performed flawlessly - something was nagging at the back of my mind, and I wanted to return to Earth.

The navigator moved us for a clear line back to Earth, and suggested we try full speed, just to see what it was, as no one was actually sure. We all agreed, after all, we were on a test flight, and others would find the data useful. I asked if we could take another look at Mars on the way back - just to get some new pictures with the high definition camera, and it was agreed.

We seemed to arrive at Mars a lot quicker than anticipated, and went into orbit. Knowing the distance we had travelled, and the time taken, it was easy to work out our speed - and that was frightening. It looked as if we had exceeded the speed of light, but more accurate calculations would have to be done to confirm that.

Somehow, Mars looked a little different - there were patches of green and brown here and there - and something shining - water? I called our geologist, Tony, to get his opinion. He took a good look, consulted his charts, and stated that this was a part of Mars which hadn't been photographed very much, and little was known about it.

Although I accepted what he said, I felt uneasy about it - surely someone must have noticed the green patches - it would have been a major event. After a long discussion, it was agreed two of us would go down, take samples and photographs, and then head for home.

The Lander touched down just short of a green patch, and suited up, we stepped out onto the Martian soil for the first time. It took only minutes to reach the green area just ahead of the Lander. It was green alright, but not like the grass of Earth - it was more like a lichen or moss, and was quite thick - almost nine centimetres in places. It covered the red Martian soil, and even encroached on some low lying boulders - and something on its surface moved. I went over and pulled the green stuff back - a small dark blue beetle-like creature scurried back under the greenery, and search as I might, I didn't find it again. Luckily, Tony had seen it too - pity we didn't get a snap of it. We walked on for a few minutes, and came to an area where the greenery had been cropped - cropped is not the right word - it had been ripped out in great chunks, some of which lay slowly withering in the dry atmosphere. Close by were some footprints - not of our making. It was of a three toed creature, and by the length between the steps, it must have been of a considerable size. As neither of us were armed, we thought it best to leave the area a bit sharpish, and return to the Lander, but before we did so, I gathered up several handfuls of the greenery, stuffing it into the specimen bag at my waist to take back with us.

Back on board, the details of what we had seen were met with astonishment, and disbelief, until the photos and the sample were shown.

When we get back to Earth, no doubt a team would be sent out to verify what we had seen, and bring back more samples for analysis.

The ship was aligned up with Earth, and the drive switched on - we were homeward bound.

The first thing which caught our attention was that we couldn't see the Space Station. We knew where it should be - and it wasn't. We sent out a radio message, but all we got back was a static hiss. Something cold ran down my back as we looked at each other - it was just possible that it had crashed back to Earth - but there had been no reply to our radio call - even from Earth.

Slowly the ship was brought in to low orbit, and then the other differences began to show up. The polar ice caps were much smaller, and the whole world seemed greener - even some of the desert areas were green. We circled Earth until we reached the place where the Space

Centre should have been - and there was no sign of it - or any other buildings. The co-ordinates were checked again and again - we hadn't made a mistake. Another orbit of Earth failed to show any works of man - it was as if he had never been. Doc broke open the emergency brandy, and we all took a good swig, and then another one, but it didn't make any difference.

Once we had got over the shock, it was decided to use the Landers to go down to the surface to see what had actually happened. With three in each Lander, we slipped away from the ship and entered the atmosphere, circling the planet to look for any signs of construction, but there were none - not even the pyramids, in fact where they should have been was covered in vegetation.

The only thing which was easily recognisable, was the Grand Canyon, and that showed up clearly - but not quite as I remembered it, somehow it wasn't deep enough.

The co-ordinates for the Space Centre were fed into the guidance systems, the Landers changed direction, and we headed for our base - or where it should have been.

We came down in an area of scrub - a few tree-like growths, but mainly what looked like small bushes, except they weren't bushes as we had known them - more like ferns. The air seemed clean and fresh, the light was bright - even too bright, it took a while for our eyes to get used to it. There didn't seem to be any insects in the air or on the ground, in fact - no life at all, apart from the weird plants.

When we got over the initial shock, we had to decide what to do. We could stay where we were, but food could be a problem - and possibly water. We could go back to the ship, which was in a stable orbit, but then what? No other planet looked as if it would support life as we knew it. Or we could head out into interstellar space, but we didn't have enough provisions to last more than a week or so, which meant we would starve before we reached another star system.

In the end, we thought the best thing to do was to find a river which went down to the sea. That would give us fresh water, and perhaps we could catch some fish for food. Using the Landers, we chose a fast flowing river, which meant it wouldn't be contaminated with salt water at high tide, and with a piece of bent wire and some thread from a nylon jacket, set about fishing. The only bait we could find was from a shell-like creature stuck on a rock at low tide. It was attached to our hook and dangled into the sea from a rocky promontory, but nothing took the bait - even after several hours.

This meant we would have to exist on shellfish and river water - God what I could do to a hamburger and chips! Using the Landers as sleeping quarters and a base, we settled in to the inevitable. Ben thought the high speed of our travel had somehow warped or twisted the time line - and God knows where we were now. It looked like two possibilities, either we had gone into the far future and Earth had reverted to a former state earlier in its life, or we had gone back into the past before the land had been colonised by animals of one sort or another. Either way, we were the only animals on the land - as far as we could tell.

It looked as if man had come and gone, or he had yet to arrive.

FROM LONG AGO

Berg Goldbloom was rummaging about in the back of an old second-hand book shop when he came across it. It had slipped down behind a row of tattered old volumes, and was covered in years of dust. It was very old, battered, and with an unpleasant smell about it - but it was intriguing.

Taking it to the old man with pebble glasses behind the desk he asked, 'How much', trying to show disinterest. The old man turned it over in his gnarled hands, shrugged twice, and settled for the price of a coffee.

Berg hurried home to his bachelor flat, grabbed a beer, and sat down to see exactly what he had bought. Although the book was of average size, it seemed to weigh very heavily in his hand, and as he turned it over, a slip of old parchment fluttered down to the floor. He picked it up, and going over to the window for more light, tried to make out what the faint old script said.

This foul thing must be burned in the hottest fire possible, and a mass said before and after the burning. Anyone who has touched this heretical evil must serve a seven day penance, with lashes, at the rising of the sun, and at its going down. After destruction by fire, the ashes are to be ground down, mixed with thrice blessed Holy Water and burned again. Anything left shall be buried in the deepest hole, the hole filled with hot stones and covered with a heavy piece of granite, which also shall be blessed.

By Order of the Cardinal

Below the last words was an almost undecipherable signature, and the remains of a deep purple wax seal.

Berg opened the book, leafing through the crinkled old parchment pages to see what all the fuss was about. There were pictures of winged dragons, some breathing fire, goblins, humans with animal heads on them, and a whole load of unpleasant and suggestive looking symbols. There were pages of what looked like recipes, but for what it didn't say, and then the interesting bit which had caught Berg's imagination in the first place. Five pages of what looked like circuit diagrams for something electronic.

Berg had always been a dab-hand with a soldering iron, making all sorts of electrical and electronic gadgets for his own amusement, so the pages sort of rang a bell with him. Although there were no recognisable conventional components or symbols, the layout looked 'electronic'. A mass of what could be crystals, wire coils, and indefinable blobs with strange squiggles on them, littered the pages, together with little bits of some strange script dotted about between the components.

After several hours and an equal number of beers, he was still none the wiser, but felt it should make sense to someone with a greater knowledge of electronics than him. Rather than hand the book over, he had the five pages photocopied, and then rang up one of his old college friends who now worked for an international electronics company.

'Hi Bob, I've found what looks like some old electronic circuits in a very old book. I can't make head or tail of them, but thought you might. Feel like a beer and a pizza this evening?'

Bob agreed to come round after work, and give it the once over.

'See what you mean, Berg - it suggests something electronic, but God knows what the components are, or what they're supposed to do. Must say, I'm interested. The only thing I can suggest is that I take each section bit by bit and try and work out what they are trying to achieve, and then using algorithms, try and stick it all together. I'll have to swap these odd looking components for the modern equivalents, and then you can build the thing up, whack on some power, and see what happens. It's going to take a day or two, but I'll get back to you if I can make any sense of it.'

They spent the rest of the evening talking over old times and giving the beer stocks a good thrashing.

Five days later, and Bob came round with the results.

'This is the strangest thing I've ever seen,' Bob said, scratching the back of his head, 'and I've seen some. The last page had me stuck for some time; it's a mass of little crystals set up in a matrix - and then I got it; it's a sort of vision screen, but it would be very low definition. What I've done is make up this little circuit board. If you plug one end into the circuit you are going to build and the other into a flat screen monitor, and if the thing picks anything up, it'll show on the screen - but don't hold your breath. I've also added two orange wires for a loudspeaker, that's if the thing makes any sounds, and another pair of white ones for a microphone, should there be anyone at the other end.'

'Do you have any idea of what it's supposed to do?' asked Berg, 'I couldn't make it out.'

'It seems to be some sort of communication device, which is surprising considering when it was drawn - they didn't know anything about electronics in those days, so where the bloke who drew it up got his information from beats me. Oh, and there's something else; you see these five coils? You'll have to wind them yourself on ferrite formers, there's no way you can buy them ready made, and the middle winding is in reverse to the other two - God knows why, it doesn't make any sense to me, but that's what's called for. These funny little blobs seem to be capacitors - couldn't work out their values exactly, so I've brought a bag of mixed ones, just plug them in and swap them around until something happens.'

'Thanks for your help, I'll let you know if it works,' said Berg. 'If you don't hear from me, you'll know it's blown up.'

'You're welcome, must be off, I've got a hot date - far too hot to miss, good luck.' And with that Bob left, leaving his version of the circuit diagram and the bag of capacitors on the table.

It took Berg several days to collect together all the components, and a further two to wind the fiddly coils, and at last he had everything ready for assembling, but of what?

It took quite a while to solder the components together, and then he wasn't really sure if he had got it right. After several checks against the circuit Bob had drawn, he plugged in the little circuit board built to drive the monitor, and added the power supply. Berg paused for a while before switching the device on, everything seemed alright, and so he took the plunge, and clicked the switch.

At first nothing happened, except for the power light to come on, and then there was a faint crackle from the loudspeaker, and the screen lit up with a faint glow.

There was only one control knob to twiddle, so he did, and the screen was suddenly filled with the usual pattern of static when no signal is present, and a low rushing noise from the speaker.

There was only one other thing to do, and that was to swap the capacitors around in their sockets. And after four swaps, the screen came to life and the hiss from the speaker died away to a faint murmur.

The scene was of a circular craggy cave of dark rock, with a strange red glow. Little wisps of smoke or steam drifted up from the floor spasmodically, and then a dark chuckle came from the speaker.

'Ahhh, Earthling, you have made contact at last, it's been a very, very long time since we last spoke. If I remember, the last time I made a visit to your world, the reception was not very nice - in fact, it was definitely hostile. Perhaps you have all had a change of mind? It looks as if it's time I paid you another visit…..'

Berg noticed a faint whiff of a sulphurous nature in the air.

A dark red figure walked into full view with stubby horns on its head and a tail which swished back and forth, and the most evil of grins…

OLD AND NEW BITS

FOR 148 YEARS old, I suppose I'm doing quite well; mind you, there aren't many of the old body parts left, apart from the main frame that is - and that's had a few tweaks here and there.

My first experience, a long time ago, of 're-building', was when my heart and liver packed up. There was a long waiting list for organs, but there was the option for a pig's liver and heart transplant on the Continent (they won't do it here) - so I took it.

Worked very well, but the liver couldn't handle the cholesterol level too well, so they put a controlling micro-chip in - that did the trick, and after a few weeks I stopped grunting.

When the new auto-cars came on the market, I got one - should have waited a bit for the bugs to be ironed out. Great idea - you just put your destination in, press the button and it takes you there - no steering, you can even read a book if you wish.

I was tanking up a motorway one day, when the car did a handbrake turn, and faced the on coming traffic. In the ensuing crash I lost both my legs, from the hip down.

The new mechanical self powered ones are just great; I can walk all day, for as far as I like, and I don't get tired. Just have to refill the tank in the fuel cell once a month.

When my eyes failed, I had them replaced with the new synthetic ones. They only worked in black and white, but at least I could see where I was going. Five years later, I upgraded to the colour vision ones; much better, although the colours are a bit garish.

Fed up with the old false teeth; so I raided the cookie jar and found just enough to try the new 'tooth bud' implants. They take some of my stem cells, do something clever with them and produce these little pellets - seen them, like little gains of rice.

Under a local anaesthetic, they make a hole in the gum down to the bone, and implant the pellets - takes a long time for the teeth to grow, but it's worth it - now got a great set of new gleaming white teeth.

When the last few wisps of hair disappeared, I tried root transplants. Didn't like it, they seemed to lay in different directions, so this meant setting them each morning with a hairdryer - fed up with that, so had a synthetic head piece fitted - brilliant! A quick rinse in the shower once a week, and it looks like new.

When I lost my right hand, I had a transplant. Trouble is, it makes rude gestures at random people. God knows why. I've had three black eyes, (luckily it didn't damage the synthetic optics), a kick in the unmentionables, and two court cases.

The colon finally packed up, as did my stomach. A plastic one was fitted (with a controlling microchip) which works quite well, except it generates copious amounts of gas - can't always control it, and it's highly flammable as I found out once when passing a lit scented candle at a house party. I had to pay for the blown out window and three women's dresses, which were badly singed.

My skin, not surprisingly at my age, was getting a bit wrinkled - to say the least of it. The latest thing on the market is 'nanobots'. They are injected into the blood stream where they collect stem cells, and then transport them to damaged tissue to affect a repair. Wish they'd been around earlier, it would have saved all those transplants.

Got myself a new girlfriend. She's young, (78) and a real goer, if you see what I mean. Since the 'nanobot' injections, I am now firing on all four cylinders, and can just about keep up. Perhaps I should have got someone a little older.

Just had the artificial feet modified. The latest thing is retractable wheels. In effect, this turns them into powered roller-skates. Knocked a few people over to begin with, but I am getting the hang of it now.

My surgeon, (who also owns the company making the controlling micro chips) suggested it would be a good idea if I had a 'master controller' fitted. This would keep an eye, so to speak, on all the others, making sure they all worked in unison.

I sometimes get the feeling I am no longer in full control - just little things, like what programmes to watch on the wall vision screen. I press the button for one program, but a different one comes up - usually science or medical based. I like jam doughnuts, but one day as I reached for one in the café, my hand refused to grasp it - moving on to grab a piece of quiche. Feeding the ducks on the local pond is quite fun (actually, they're artificial ones, but very realistic) but the wheeled feet sometimes won't stop, and go on to the permanent fairground just down the road, where we try out all the rides until the tokens run out. I suppose it's a small price to pay for still being around.

The other day I noticed I was being followed around by what I can only call a hideous old hag. I'm not being unkind, she really is the pits. Lank hair, skin wrinkled like a prune, half her teeth missing, and a distinct unpleasant body odour when the wind is in the wrong direction. Keep meeting her - in shops - on the transports - she even sat next to me in the cinema once - had to put up with it as there were no other empty seats. God, it's a drag.

She always greets me with a toothy grin, and mumbles on in some foreign tongue I have never heard of - or her larynx needs replacing. She must have had quite a few bits and pieces replaced to keep going at that age - maybe she did it on the cheap, using rejected items off the internet.

If I see her coming, I usually drop my wheels, and speed off. Now the bitch has had wheels added to her replacement legs - must be the latest ones - I can't out pace her.

Most people still have mobile phones, although the new communication system favoured by the young is to have an implant in the back of your skull, so there's no need to trundle around with a physical phone in your hand. So I got one.

I got a call in the middle of the night - frightened the life out of me. This croaky voice bleated on about how wonderful I was, etc. etc. Somehow she must have got my code number, and extended her nefarious operations into the night hours. She'd had some work done on her vocal cords, as I could just about understand her. I changed my code, and a few nights later the calls began again.

Had a chat with the local police chief about it - he did his best to hide his mirth, but failed miserably. I had the chip removed. Sometimes the old technology is best, I can switch the bloody thing off.

Had a chat with a friend, who said he thought something else was taking over his life - he's had everything fitted you can get, and then some. Same sort of thing - he wants to do one thing, but his body does something else - not often, but enough to be noticed.

Saw the bitch again yesterday; had some repair work done by the look of it. She's put some weight on, and some of the wrinkles have filled out - got a new set of teeth, and a wig. She must have fallen in the duck pond - looks a lot cleaner, and the smell has gone - unless my nose has packed up - must get it checked.

'Oh God, something has taken over again. Find myself putting on best clothes, and hurrying out of the house. Just had a phone call from HER - 'meet me at 2:30pm, outside the fertility clinic …Oh God.

THE END

If you have enjoyed this book, please consider leaving a review on Amazon. It would mean a lot to us.

Other books by David Reynolds-Moreton

The Seed Garden
Extreme Difference
Exchange Rate
The Martian Enigma
The Single Twin
Transplant
Greenways
The Tribe
The Sweepers
Of wood, Metal, and Glass
Enslavement
Flight of the Tristan
Divergence
Life Force
Anthology of Futures
Light Quest
Intervention
The Power Seeds
Inheritance
Zuki
Fully Guaranteed

Audio Books

Transplant | Greenways | The Tribe | The Seed Garden

Scan the QR code below to discover these titles online

About the Author

"Back in 1998 I was commenting to a friend that I didn't go much on so called modern Science Fiction. It didn't seem as good or as interesting as the adventures stories written by the old masters of sci-fi – Clarke, Russell, Pohl, Asimov, Heinlein etc. His reaction was 'well, write your own then' – As I already had an idea at the back of my mind, I did. After printing up ten copies and binding them (hardback) they were passed around among like minded friends – and then came the request for more of the same! Again and again. Only one problem – I was spending too much time printing and binding and not writing, which I enjoy. Getting into 'print' is difficult – if not impossible – so I chose the 'eBook' route. I would recommend it to anyone who likes writing, and has a story to tell."

David (aka D.B) Reynolds-Moreton is a retired research and development engineer who lives in Devon, England with his wife. You can read a short biography of his life and adventures in science at :

www.sci-fi-cafe.com/david-reynolds-moreton

www.ingramcontent.com/pod-product-compliance
Lightning Source LLC
Chambersburg PA
CBHW030810190726
48285CB00003B/1105